# Courtin' Dory

## SARAH RICHMOND

First Edition: Brides of Serendipity Copyright © 2008 Sarah Richmond
Revised Edition, *Courting Dory* copyright 2018 by Sarah Richmond

First Electronic Edition; ISBN: 978-0-9861671-3-3
Print Edition: ISBN-13: 978-1-7332573-0-5

# Dedication

*This book is dedicated to Avery Allen*

# Acknowledgements

Just outside Fallon, Nevada on Route 50 on the way to Carson City, stands a Nevada Historical Marker for Ragtown. It is all that remains of the once thriving town. The people who lived there were as diverse as the American landscape. They are now part of American history. My hope is they will be remembered for their hard work, physical and moral courage and family loyalty. Together, they built a nation.

Many thanks to the Fallon, Nevada Tourism Office for their help and interest in this project. Also to the Mark Twain Bookstore in Virginia City, Nevada for their suggestions. For more information about the State of Nevada and the interesting places to see there, please try **www.travelnevada.com**.

# Courtin' Dory

## NEVADA TERRITORY: 1854

# Chapter One

DORY WATKINS' MA took bad sick coming across the Forty Mile desert the summer of '54. Dory would be eighteen come September and considered full grown by most and she decided she would stay behind in Ragtown and tend to her ma. Her pa reckoned otherwise.

"I ain't splitting up the family," he said as he rubbed smelly salve on Old Buck's harness sores.

"But Pa."

Seth Watkins quelled her with a stern look. He didn't like anybody contradicting him, least ways a girl.

"Now Dory," he said. "Don't think I haven't been giving the situation some thought. We'll stay here in Ragtown until the next wagon train passes through in six weeks. Your ma will be able to travel by then."

Her ma had been taken by the fever. Dory knew another kind of fever burned in her pa's gullet. Gold fever, folks called the powerful desire that'd set them out on the trail West.

"The land in California needs claiming," she reasoned. "You and the boys can continue on and build us a house

1

before winter sets in. Ma and I won't be alone. There'll be plenty of good folks traveling from back east in the next train."

Pa considered for a moment and then shook his head. "You're too young to be taking on such a big responsibility."

Dory knew her pa's objections were more than her tender years. It wasn't in him to leave the women unprotected.

"I just walked from Ulysses to this very spot," she said, crossing her arms. "I've stood up to more hardship than most see in a lifetime. We survived sickness and rattlers and even an Injun scouting party. I grew up and you weren't even watching."

Her father brushed off his hands. She saw something she hadn't seen since they left their farm in Kansas. A smile spread across her pa's chiseled face.

"How do you expect to handle a team of horses?" he asked.

Dory had an answer ready. "There'll be plenty of menfolk coming with the next party. There'll be one or two who will be willing to give two ladies a hand."

Pa replaced the lid on the tin of salve. His hands were as brown as beans and tough as shoe leather. Dory knew every one of her family had endured more than a body could take but the biggest burden had fallen to her pa. She couldn't let him give up what they'd all worked for since leaving their ill-fated farm. Not if she was able to take on this responsibility.

"Ma can't travel and the wagon train won't wait," she said. "We can't loose the land we've all sacrificed for. We'll all be reunited in the land of milk and honey."

Her pa examined her. She'd spoken the words that he'd

used to describe California a dozen times since he and ma had first decided to leave their family and friends. They were headed for the land of milk and honey, he'd told them all, the land of promise.

"Adam will stay with your ma."

Dory grimaced. Pa always turned to her brother to rely on and Adam was only a year older. Adam had driven the team on the second wagon. Adam was sent out to hunt game when the wagon train stopped for the evening. Dory's job had been to gather buffalo chips for the evening's fire.

"You'll need Adam's help to build the cabin," Dory said. "Why leave him behind when I can manage just fine?"

Pa was quiet for a long minute. Dory shifted uneasily. She'd argued her best and Pa's decision would be final.

"We'll leave the deciding to Ma," he said.

Dory nodded. Ma's health had always been their first concern. Talking this over with Ma showed he'd seen some sense to what Dory'd been saying.

"I'll meet up with you in the wagon as soon as I take care of the horses." He led Buck down to the Carson River where he could fill his belly on some sweet grass.

Her pa spoke with a sadness Dory wished she could erase. He'd grown serious as if there wasn't any joy in him ever since they'd left their dried-up farm, the ground so hard nothing would grow. He'd borrowed money from Ma's brother to buy oxen and a second wagon. Pa hated to be indebted and was itching to start panning for gold so he could repay his obligations.

Dory had faith that her family would be fine once they all arrived in California. Pa would find gold and there'd be money to spare. A separation would only be temporary.

Hopefully, her pa would realize she was strong-willed like him.

Adam rode up on his chestnut gelding, an eighteenth birthday present from Pa last year. He'd gone west looking for game and Dory was happy to see him come back empty-handed. He dismounted and handed over the reins to Dory.

"You take care of your own horse," Dory said, refusing the reins. "I've got my own chores to attend to."

"Don't be so sour-faced," Adam told her. "You'll be wrinkled up before your time. No man will have you looking like a prune."

Dory held her ground. Adam gathered the reins and shook his head.

"Don't be wandering too far," she called after him. "There's plenty of chores to do here in camp."

"I don't take my orders from you," Adam replied and he led his horse away.

Dory climbed into the back of the Conestoga wagon. Their two wagons were apart from the others in the train on account of Ma's illness. The town was far enough away to keep the contagion from spreading.

Adam riled her but she wouldn't let Ma see. She wouldn't cause her ma any worry if she could help it.

Ma looked fragile lying in the featherbed, padded by pillows. Dory had been so scared when her ma had stayed put the day before yesterday. She couldn't remember a time when Ma wasn't up before the others, with a fire blazing and breakfast frying up in the pan.

They'd lost two others in the train from the illness, the Wilkinson's baby and Mrs. Johnson. The rest of them had been spared. Why Dory hadn't taken sick, she didn't rightly know. Providence had other plans for her, she reckoned.

Death had stalked them every step of the way. Many a traveler had been claimed by sickness. Others by accidents. Some just plumb wore out. The roadside coming west was a graveyard for those who'd passed the same way and fallen, their final resting places marked by wooden crosses. Dory considered the pioneer trail sacred ground.

They'd stopped in Ragtown. This small settlement, they'd been told, had sprouted up because of the need for fresh stock and supplies before the wagon trains continued on across the mountains and into California.

When she first set eyes on what was considered a town, she was dismayed at the ramshackle place. No more than a jumble of dirty tents, lean-tos and a few wood-framed structures thrown together in a hurry. The most prominent building was a saloon. The locals had given the town the name Ragtown, strangely enough, because of the fresh washing spread out on the tufts of sagebrush.

The name suited the place. It didn't rightly look like a town with any permanence. She knew with certainty Ragtown was a place decent folks passed through on their way to something better.

Dory grasped her ma's hand to give comfort but also to see if the fever was still there. This morning, Ma's hand was cold and clammy. Dory decided her condition would need watching.

"Where's your pa?" Ma asked, her eyes half-open and not looking anywhere in particular.

"He'll be right along. We've a question we want to ask."

Her ma tried to raise herself. Dory adjusted her pillow and her ma slumped back against it, clearly exhausted.

"A family meeting?" she asked. She turned to look at

Dory.

"Yes, that's right."

Her pa poked his head inside the wagon. "You awake?"

Ma smiled. She was always generous with her smiles but this morning her smile was riveted on Pa's hopeful face.

"Feeling any better?" he said as he climbed inside.

"Some."

Ma wasn't the type to complain and she wasn't about to add to the burden Pa already carried.

He nodded. "That's good."

Pa removed his hat and ran his big hand over his head. His hair needed cutting, a chore that fell to Ma. Neither said a word about it.

"Dory, go fetch the boys. This is a family meeting and they need to be here," Ma said.

Dory left reluctantly. Her ma was always saying that Dory was growing up faster than seemed possible. She wanted to state her case that she could manage for them both before Pa had a chance to convince Ma otherwise.

She couldn't find Adam but she didn't have far to go to find her two younger brothers. They watched a young man exercise a young horse on the end of a rope next to the blacksmith's tent.

"Lookie," her youngest brother shouted out to her. "He's crossed a mustang with a plow horse."

Dory thought the animal was the ugliest critter she'd ever laid eyes on.

"He aims to sell him to the folks who need fresh stock," her brother continued.

Dory didn't see how the animal could pull a wagon. It wasn't as tall or stocky as their team. Buck stood eighteen hands and had no trouble hauling a load. From the look of this horse, he was as flighty as a jaybird. Now old Buck had a gentle disposition and one that just about anybody could handle.

Besides, most westerners preferred oxen for pulling the heavy loads. Pa used three yoke to pull the big wagon.

"Come along, boys. Ma wants you."

The man pulled the horse to a stop.

"His name is Harley Jacobs," her brother said, ignoring what she'd said. It wasn't easy being the only girl in the family.

"Harley, this here is my sister Dory."

Harley Jacobs touched the brim of his hat. "Howdy."

The wrangler was tall and skinny. He wore buckskin chaps, a blue flannel shirt and a pale lavender kerchief around his sun-freckled neck. He wasn't much older than Dory.

"Nice to meet you," Dory replied cordially. "Do as I say, boys."

Her brothers moved away from the man and horse with their heads down, kicking at the dirt.

"I'll show you a few rope tricks when you're finished with your business," Harley said.

The boys' eyes brightened and they turned around, nodding their heads eagerly.

"Can we, Dory?"

Dory looked at their new friend. He drew up the rope into a big circle, a smile the size of the territory on his face.

"If it's not any trouble," she replied.

"No trouble, ma'am." Again he touched his hat. His gaze intertwined with hers.

Dory felt as if she'd been caught with her petticoat showing but that was foolishness. She started back for the wagon, both cheeks burning.

MA WOULDN'T HEAR of Pa waiting around for her to get back on her feet. She saw right away the wisdom in Dory's plan and them staying behind in Ragtown. They'd leave with the next train passing through.

Pa didn't say much after that. Dory knew how the decision just about tore him apart. He and Ma hadn't been separated since the day they'd married over twenty years ago. As much as she hated to see his heart broken, Dory understood the necessity of him and the boys moving out with their party.

Pa'd have a new home built and ready when Dory and Ma arrived six weeks later. They'd have just enough time to settle before winter blew in.

Dory would give him no cause to regret the decision.

The morning of their departure, Dory helped pack the bigger wagon, handing up a side of bacon wrapped in a burlap bag.

"Best steer clear of town," Pa told her. "There's folks there prone to high living."

"Yes, sir." She'd heard talk about men who'd kill another man over a game of cards and the shameless hussies who followed them from camp to camp. "You've got nothing to fear on that score. Me and Ma will stay down here by the river where it's cooler and the water's plentiful. I'll tend to her and we'll be ready when that next train comes through."

Pa didn't look at her. "I know you will, daughter. Mind, if you need anything, the Jacobs are decent folks, and the Millers over at the mercantile, and Doc and his

Mrs. They'll see to anything you might need."

Dory assured him she would seek out the others in Ragtown who were like them.

He finished storing the supplies and eased out of the back of the wagon. "We'll be reunited in the land of milk and honey."

"Sooner than you reckon," she replied. Her eyes glistened. She hadn't wanted to cry but she couldn't help herself. With a quick sniff and a wipe of the back of her hand across her face, she stood on her toes and kissed her pa on his cheek.

The Watkinses weren't given to sloppy farewells. Pa least of all. He came from sturdy Calvinist stock and had no use for tearful goodbyes.

Her pa called to the boys. Her brothers scrambled into the back of the wagon. The excitement of the adventure was plain on their faces.

Adam mounted his horse.

"You take good care of Ma and yourself," he said.

"You know I will," she replied.

Her brother's face was etched with concern. She hadn't thought it possible that he had a caring bone in his body for anybody but himself.

Dory smiled to reassure him. It didn't seem possible after all these years living in his shadow that she was finally being given an adult-size responsibility. She sensed Adam appreciated the importance of this moment.

Pa took his seat in the front. He picked up the reins and shook them without further *adieu*. The team moved forward. Dory stepped out of the way.

The other wagons were already on the heavily rutted trail raising dust. Her family's wagon pulled in behind. Adam rode alongside. The boys looked out the back hanging on to the heavy canvas and waved.

Dory waved back. She kept waving until she couldn't see their bright, eager faces any longer.

# Chapter Two

D ORY HAD PLENTY to keep her occupied. Her primary concern was restoring her ma's health. Old Buck and his partner Gussie had to be cared for. Pa left enough money with her and a word to the blacksmith to have the team fitted with a new set of shoes before the next wagon arrived. She'd make sure the horses fattened up on the sweet grass that grew along the banks of the Carson River.

The land around these parts was nothing to crow about. Some scraggily old cottonwoods grew along the riverbank, and the ground was dotted with sagebrush and chaparral. The land wasn't suited for farming and she was farming stock.

As she climbed into the back of the wagon to bring Ma some water, she was thinking how different California would be.

What Dory saw startled her. Her ma tossed and turned and her face had broken out in tiny beads of sweat. Dory knelt by the bed and felt her forehead. Ma moved away as if Dory's touch was unbearable but Dory could tell she was burning up.

"Go fetch the doctor," her ma said weakly.

Dory hated leaving her but Dr. McKinnon would know what Ma needed. She jumped down from the wagon. The town seemed a fair piece ahead.

Not taking the time to put on her bonnet, she ran up

the slope to town. The morning heat and dust pulled her up short. Her breath was ragged and her throat hurt but there was no time to recover. She started off again.

When she reached the first lopsided building, she wanted to rest again. The shade gave her comfort but she didn't stop this time. She continued on up the deeply rutted road that served as the main street.

The town was made up of two parts. The mercantile and a few other businesses on one side with a boardwalk made out of rough-sawn wood connecting them. On the other side, a two story post and beam building stood by its lonesome. Piano music drifted out through fancy swinging doors along with bursts of laughter and loud talking. Men were drinking and it wasn't even noon.

She averted her eyes and quickened her pace until she reached a log cabin with curtains in the window. A shingle with the doc's name identified the home.

A woman answered the door. She was Ma's age and wore a white apron. Her dark brown hair was pinned into a neat bun at the back of her head. She fiddled nervously with the top button of her shirtwaist dress as she waited to hear what Dory wanted.

"I'm Dory Watkins. My ma and me are camped down by the Carson." The words tumbled out of her as she tried to catch her breath.

The fear of contagion was clear in the woman's wide-eyed expression. She stepped back to stand partially hidden behind the door.

"Is Doc McKinnon home?" Dory asked, not taking offense. The sickness scared the bravest of souls.

"My husband's out at the Rocking J.," the woman said. "One of their men broke his leg."

"Ma's burning up and needs a doctor real bad," Dory

cried. Panic coated her words.

"He'll be back as soon as he's able," Mrs. McKinnon replied.

Dory couldn't wait. She thanked Mrs. McKinnon and asked her to make sure the doc came down to their camp as soon as possible.

"I'll tell him about your mother," the lady reassured her.

Biting her lip, Dory fled the way she'd come. She didn't know what she was going to do. She didn't know how to control the fever that raged through her ma's body.

When she reached the boardwalk, she met up with Harley Jacobs riding a big red horse.

"Where are you off to in such a hurry?" he asked, friendly like.

She resented his easy going ways. Her heart was too full of terror to exchange pleasantries.

"My ma is bad," she said. "The sickness has put a fever in her. I've just been to Doc McKinnon's but he's mending a cowhand's broken leg out at the Rocking J."

Harley's grin faded. "Can I help?"

"I can't let you. The fever's already killed two in our party."

"I'll be careful," he said. He reached out with an open hand. "Come on up. Riding will get us there faster."

She grasped his hand and hooked her shoe in the stirrup. He hauled her up and she swung her leg over the animal's wide withers. She tucked her skirt underneath her.

"Hang on," he said.

Harley Jacobs didn't have much meat on his bones, she thought as she grabbed hold of his shirt but he wore that lavender kerchief and she was partial to the color.

He didn't waste any time. They started off at a trot

down the middle of the street. The raggedy old tents flapped in the breeze as they passed but the horse didn't spook. Harley kept a tight rein. Despite the bumpy ride, Dory was grateful.

They crossed the dried-up field at a canter. Her hair worked loose and blew in all directions. She didn't dare let go of him to clear the tangles off her face. They reached the wagon in no time. She slid off the horse hanging on to Harley's strong arm.

Harley dismounted and staked his horse to a hank of scrub brush.

Dory climbed into the back of the wagon and Harley followed. Ma looked no better. The fever had reddened her face in splotches and fresh beads of sweat had broke out across her brow.

Ma tried to sit up when she saw Harley stooped over at the end of the bed, his hat clutched in his hand.

"Did I hear Indians about?" her ma asked frantically.

Dory stayed her with a gentle hand. "No, I haven't seen none."

Ma's frightened gaze was fixed on Harley.

"That's Harley Jacobs," Dory said. "He's come to help."

Ma grabbed Dory's wrist. There was no strength in her grip. "Don't let them steal our horses."

"Don't you worry," Dory replied softly. "I won't."

Dory had never been so afraid. Ma didn't seem to know where she was. Dory looked at Harley. "I've got to get this fever down. Do you think we could take her out of the wagon and put her in the river?"

Harley squashed his hat on his head. "I expect so if you think it'll help."

"I don't know what else to do," she said.

Harley lifted Ma up as tender as if she was a newborn babe. He carried her out of the wagon while Dory prayed. She prayed that God wouldn't take Ma from her. She prayed that putting her in the cooling water of the Carson was the right thing to do.

Harley strode out into the lazy water, boots and all. Dory did the same. He lowered her ma into the fast flowing stream. He cradled Ma's head and Dory held her feet together and the nightgown fast around her legs. The cottonwoods along the banks provided precious little shade but the sparkling water was cold.

"You're going to be all right," she told her mother, who looked as helpless as a kitten. Her ma didn't respond as the water rushed over her.

Ma's nightgown soaked through revealing her privates. Even though there was little modesty traveling by wagon train like they'd done, Ma was a modest woman. Harley kept his gaze on the muddy banks of the river. Dory appreciated that he wouldn't cause her or her ma unnecessary embarrassment.

Her mother's lips turned blue and she trembled.

"I guess that's enough," Dory told Harley.

He picked Ma up and sloughed out of the water. River water dripped from his pant legs and Ma's nightgown as they made their way back. When they reached the wagon, Dory dried Ma off the best she could and wrapped her in a blanket.

They settled her ma in her bed with extra blankets. Ma looked like there wasn't any blood left in her. Every bit of her had gone as white as a sheet.

"I'll go see if the doctor has come back," Harley said.

When Dory turned to say thank you, Harley had already gone.

THE NEXT MORNING, as Dory gathered brush for a campfire, Harley Jacobs rode up on his red horse with a pair of dead prairie hens tied to his saddle.

"Howdy," he said in his friendly way. He touched his hat and grinned. What he was always grinning about, Dory couldn't say.

"Morning, Harley."

"Just stopped by to see how your ma was doing."

"She's better. Doc says the cold water bath did her good."

"I'm glad to hear so."

"Thank you for your help."

His gaze was as sweet as honey. "I was glad to."

There was a moment of awkwardness, a silence that was uncomfortable. He pulled a package wrapped in brown paper out of his saddlebag. "My ma asked me to bring this over. She sends her regards."

He handed the parcel to her. She removed the string to reveal a loaf of baked bread.

"Tell your ma thank you. I don't think I've ever seen a finer loaf of bread."

He untied the hens and she took them as well.

"You must be a good shot," she said, looking over the hens with a practiced eye. "I don't see any blood."

"I didn't shoot them. I kinda snuck up on them."

She looked up at him to see if he was joshing her but there was no telling with him.

His smile just got bigger.

Harley leaned on his pommel. His easy manner made Dory self-conscious. She'd little experience with the ways of men outside her kin. She used to tag along with the neighbor boys back home when they all went to the fishing pond and she could tell a good yarn with the best of them. None of them had googly-eyed her like Harley Jacobs did.

She remembered her manners. "Won't you stay for a cup of coffee?"

"Don't mind if I do," Harley replied and he dismounted in an effortless manner.

She admired his easy confidence around horseflesh.

Dory stacked her bundle of brush in the fire ring. She'd been in charge of keeping the fire ever since they'd started out from Kansas. She'd collected plenty of buffalo chips along the trail and didn't care if she ever found another one.

With Harley watching, she grew even more self-conscious. Harley helped her build a six foot high pile of brush on top of some greasewood they'd left over from their trek across the Forty Mile. She dragged a match across a rock. The flame burst red hot and she threw it into the pile. The dry brush caught quickly.

Harley sat himself on a flat rock and watched the fire crackle and pop. She added broken up branches from a dead cottonwood. It wouldn't be long and they'd have good coals for cooking.

"You been out here long?" she asked.

"A couple of years," he answered.

"Where you from?"

"We come out from Missouri originally. My dad has no truck with the secessionists." He added a twig to the fire.

"My pa says that nothing'll come of such talk."

Harley nodded but didn't look convinced. "Where're you folks from?"

"We're plains folk out of Kansas. Our farm just dried

up. So Pa packed up my brothers, Ma and me. We're headed for California. My pa says there's riches to be found in California, more money than a body could spend in one lifetime."

Harley stared into the fire. "I've never been but I've heard the same."

"What keeps you in Ragtown?" she asked.

"Me and Dad meant to do some freighting between here and the El Dorado. There's money to be made selling goods to those who seek those riches."

"That's a lofty ambition," Dory replied.

Harley looked up at her. There was pain in his eyes. "The only ambition I ever had was to be the kind of man my dad was."

She caught the past tense. "He's gone?"

"Dad passed last winter." She heard the misery in his voice, the loss he hadn't yet recovered from.

"I'm sorry for your pa's passing."

"Thank you." He rested his arms on his knees and folded his hands.

She liked what he'd said about his pa. She thought about her own pa and what a good man he was. Her brothers had mighty tall shoes to fill. Harley Jacobs wanted to do the same. Dory reckoned he had the makings of a good man. A warmth spread through her that had nothing to do with the fire.

"The freighting business must be hard work." She sat down next to him.

His expression changed. His eyes sparkled in the fire-light and a smile came quickly. "It sure is but I've got some ideas on how to make it easier."

"How?"

"I crossed the mustangs roaming wild in these parts

with a draft horse. A mustang ain't much to look at but they're sure-footed and tough as the country they were born to. Put one of them together with the strength of a Belgian and you have one sturdy animal for pulling a wagon." He spoke with enthusiasm and his whole face lit up because he believed in what he said.

Dory felt his excitement as if it were her own. "My pa says when opportunity comes a knocking, it's important to be there to open the door."

"Your pa sounds like a man with an opinion on many things," Harley replied.

"Well, I suppose I talk about him 'cause I miss him so."

"That'd be natural."

Dory nodded. No doubt Harley was thinking the same about his own pa.

"You mean to do all this by yourself?" she asked.

Harley picked up another twig and flung it into the glowing embers. "I got a partner. He and my dad started the business."

She sensed there was something not right between the partner and Harley but she didn't press. He was looking out toward town. He had a vision of the future, no doubt. She couldn't see anything but ramshackle huts and wind-whipped tents.

Dory stood. She ladled water into the coffee pot and added dried chicory. She set the pot on a flat rock next to the heat.

"What this place could use is some trees," she said. "I don't suppose the kind of trees we had back home would have a chance of growing out here. Can you imagine tall oaks and elms along the main street providing shade?"

Harley turned to face her. His gaze stirred a longing in

her that she must resist.

"I don't know but changes are coming," he replied. "Good changes."

He was gawking at her like a schoolboy. Her heart hopped like a jackrabbit. She was aware of something happening between them. Not a friendship, nor a schoolgirl crush on a boy. This strong feeling was between a man and a woman.

She had to admit the feeling made her wary.

"So you mean to stay on here?"

"Yes, ma'am. I mean to carry on what my dad started."

Dory believed Harley would do exactly what he'd said. He wasn't shy of hard work and he knew the risks better than most, she reckoned.

"Nothing would change your mind about leaving here?" she asked.

He shook his head. The coffee began to boil.

She decided his pa dying as he'd done might've pulled a lesser man down, made him back off from all that lay ahead. Harley wasn't that kind.

"I'm in charge of taking care of my ma," she said proudly. "When the next train pulls through, we mean to join up."

"You've taken on a big responsibility," he said.

She squared her shoulders. "I'll have you know I'm capable."

"I can see you are." His eyes gleamed merrily which should've riled her but didn't.

She poured him a tin cup full of coffee. "Sorry, I don't have any sugar or milk."

He reached up. "I like it this way just fine."

She handed it over. There was a brief touch of his

hand. She jumped, spilling the hot liquid on his thumb. Embarrassment choked off her words but Harley didn't seem to notice. He transferred the cup to his other hand, shook off the drops and then took a gulp.

Dory heard her name being called. "My ma needs me."

He nodded at the tent. "You'd better go see what she wants."

"I'd better," she replied. He took another gulp and threw the remaining drops of coffee to the side. "I best leave you to your work."

He stood. He was a head taller and skinny as a pike. Her heart fluttered like a newborn chick.

She made no move to leave. He seemed glued to the spot where he stood. She wondered if he would kiss her. The way he was looking at her, she reckoned he wanted to bad enough.

Instead, he touched the brim of his hat. "Goodbye, Dory."

"Goodbye." She watched him mount his horse. He turned the animal's head and gave her one last look.

He'd carried Ma down to the river and brought them plump hens and a loaf of bread. He tamed wild horses. He most likely could do anything he set his mind to. She reckoned he was a special kind of man. Her feelings for him ran pure and true.

She poured her mother a tin cup full of coffee and tucked Mrs. Jacob's bread under her arm.

"Did I hear voices?" Ma asked as Dory climbed aboard the wagon. Ma seemed stronger this morning. She didn't cough or wheeze like she'd done for the past couple of days. In fact, her breathing was steady which surely was a sign of improvement.

Dory was thankful.

"Harley stopped by," Dory answered. "Look what he brought." She showed her ma the loaf of bread.

"What a treat," Ma said.

"Think you could eat some?"

"Maybe a little." Ma pushed herself up into a sitting position. The gray color had left her, replaced by the washed-out color of someone who'd suffered a great deal.

"Who is this Harley?" Ma asked.

"The fella from town," Dory answered casually, putting the bread and coffee down on the brass bound trunk next to the bed. "He carried you down to the river yesterday."

Ma crinkled her brows. "I don't remember."

"I'll cut the bread." Her ma never was content to be idle. She swung her bare legs over the side of the bed. If it was up to Ma, she'd be helping with the chores. Ma didn't get far. She bent over like a woman at the end of her days. The exertion of sitting up had taken a big toll. Dory helped her sit back against the pillow.

"You stay put a little while longer," Dory said. "The coffee's fresh made and I'll cut you a piece of bread."

"That'd be fine," Ma replied.

Dory handed her the tin cup. Ma grasped the cup by the handle and sipped the brew.

"Is it all right?" Dory asked.

"As good as mine," Ma replied.

Dory smiled inside and out. She sliced the bread and handed over a piece. Ma took it. She ate small bites, the first food she'd managed to keep down in several days.

Dory cut a slice for herself. She took a bite and chewed. The bread was soft and tasted good, and so much better than any bread they'd made over a fire.

Even the effort of eating wore Ma out and her hand dropped to the quilt, and the leftover bread dropped to the floor of the wagon.

"Goodness me," Ma said. "Look what I've done."

"Don't you worry, I'll take care of it." Dory took the cup and picked up the bread and set them back on the trunk.

"So you made a friend," Ma said, brushing off crumbs from her gown.

Dory fought a blush creeping up her face. She'd curl up and die if Ma ever guessed what she was feeling for Harley Jacobs.

"Not a friend, exactly."

Ma had a ready smile handy. It did Dory's heart good to see her in better spirits.

Harley's visit with that mouthwatering loaf of bread had done wonders.

"As soon as I'm better, you and I will go pay a call on Harley's ma and thank her and her boy for their hospitality."

"Yes, Ma. It surely was a kindness sending over the freshly baked bread. That's not all. He brought us a pair of prairie hens for our supper."

"I'd like to meet your young man," Ma replied.

"Oh, Ma, he's not my young man."

Ma closed her eyes. She looked peaceful.

Dory straightened the quilt. Her ma'd already guessed at Dory's being sweet on Harley. There was no hiding anything from her.

"I'll leave you to rest for a spell," she said. She picked up the bread and Ma's cup and left the wagon wondering how Ma knew.

# Chapter Three

D ORY DIDN'T SEE Harley for the rest of the day. She needed to do chores that never seemed to be finished. She took out the big iron pot and heated water for laundry. She scrubbed the faded calico and sun-bleached gingham against the tin washboard with lye soap, which left her hands red and blistered. Then she spread the clean clothes on the tufts of sage and black brush like everybody else in Ragtown did.

She made soup using the fat hens Harley had brought over. The broth seemed to help restore Ma's energy.

"I'd like to sit outside for a spell," Ma declared after she'd taken down half a cup.

Dory knew there'd be no keeping her ma in the wagon once she had a mind to leave so she hefted one of the kitchen chairs out of the back of the wagon and set it by the fire ring.

With a hand on Dory's shoulder, Ma stepped down from the tailgate. She looked around her. Her gaze rested on the mountains. "That's the direction your pa and the boys headed off to?"

"That's right," Dory replied. "They should be about halfway to the El Dorado by now."

"I reckon so," Ma said.

"I miss them."

"So do I."

"Won't be long and we'll be on our way," Dory said cheerfully.

Ma smiled. There was weakness in her and her coloring wasn't right but Dory recognized the inner peace that came through in her smile. A calm that'd helped the family through harrowing times.

Ma made her way to the chair and took her seat. She seemed content despite the heat. Dory was thankful that Ma's strength returned faster than seemed possible. She sat down on a flat rock beside her.

"Your pa's horses are putting on weight already. They'll be in good fettle to pull our wagon when the time comes."

Dory agreed. The grass had been a blessing.

Otherwise, she'd never seen a more inhospitable place. No trees grew except the sorry cottonwoods and they weren't good for much shade. The small amounts of green grass would soon be used up. The only other living creatures were snakes and lizards whose slithering ways startled Dory out of her wits and a few birds calling out along the banks of the Carson.

How the people of Ragtown eked out a living remained a mystery to her. Why anyone would want to stay here was beyond her understanding.

They talked about Pa and the boys and how long before they'd send word that they'd arrived safely. Dory couldn't help but worry. She suspected her ma did too. So much could happen crossing those mountains.

Dory steered the conversation to what they'd do once they arrived in California. Pa and the boys would build a fine house. They talked about how they'd spend the gold that they'd find on their claim.

Ma wanted a store-bought stove to cook meals on and

to keep the house warm come winter. Dory wished for a pair of soft kid gloves and a new bonnet trimmed with Spanish lace.

They talked of how the next wagon train would be here in a matter of weeks and they'd be on their way.

"Maybe tomorrow we'll pay a call on Mrs. Jacobs and Harley," Ma said.

Such a notion seemed to cheer her ma and Dory would like nothing better. "If you feel up to it."

"We'll see in the morning, won't we?" She made a wobbly attempt to stand. Dory hurried to her feet and stood beside her.

"Goodness, my legs are like jelly," Ma said, trying to make light of her weakness.

"Maybe you've gone and overdone it," Dory replied.

"I'll be just fine. Sitting out here has done me a world of good."

Dory wasn't so sure as she helped her ma move slowly back to their wagon.

TWO DAYS LATER Ma appeared ready for a stroll into town. After they'd washed up the breakfast dishes, Dory and her ma put on their Sunday best bonnets. Before the illness, Ma had a spring in her step. Today, each step seemed to take more effort than she could muster.

Dory worried that she'd never be recovered enough to make the journey across the sprawling mountain pass that separated them from California and Pa and the boys.

When they reached the edge of town, Ma hesitated, her gaze on the jumble of tumbled-down shacks and dirty tents. This was a rag town, all right, Dory thought. Not a real town at all, leastways not like the towns back home.

The saloon caught Ma's attention and she stiffened.

"Come along, Dory," her ma said firmly.

Dory hadn't told her ma that she'd come alone to fetch the doc that day when Ma had been burning up with the fever. It didn't seem worth burdening her ma with the details, especially since Dory had managed to find the doc's house without any trouble.

She'd promised Pa that she'd steer clear of certain folks. If a drunken cowhand came stumbling out of that saloon, Dory knew better than to engage him in a conversation.

She'd discovered on the trail that most cowhands were respectful toward ladies, but drink could make a man mean. Many a story of gunfights had been told around the campfires. This was a lawless land where men settled their differences among themselves. Often the right of the matter boiled down to who was fastest with a six-shooter.

Ma slowed as they climbed the steps to the boardwalk. Dory took hold of her arm. They took their time and Dory pointed out the merchandise crowding the window of the mercantile. Ma stopped to take a look. There was a pretty bolt of yellow calico in the window. A sign showed eggs priced at twelve dollars each and a pound sack of wheat flour went for fifteen.

"Can you believe those prices?" Dory asked, amazed.

"Doesn't matter," her ma replied. "We've no need."

Pa had left her with money for the blacksmith and little else and Dory had no place to wear a new dress anyway, but still she cast her gaze at the bolt of yellow cloth with longing.

"At these prices, the man who owns the mercantile will be the richest man in the territory," she told her ma.

Ma nodded.

A man came outside carrying a broom. He wore a stained apron. His black hair was as straight as the broom straw and parted in the middle. She saw a flash of recognition in his eyes.

"Good morning," Ma said.

The fear of contagion was still evident in the man's wary gaze. He bowed slightly and retreated into the store.

They continued on, Ma's head held high. Two ladies approached carrying baskets.

Ma smiled as they passed but they didn't speak. She didn't seem upset or offended.

"It takes time for them to get used to newcomers," Ma said in her knowing way.

Dory hurt for her ma anyways. It wasn't her fault she got sick.

The Jacobs' house was a considerable distance from the center of town. The place was built of cedar logs just like Dr. McKinnon's house. By the time they arrived at the front door, Dory was overheated and thirsty.

Mrs. Jacobs met them at the door. She was dressed in a black gown ruffled at the wrists. A streak of white hair stood out on her head of raven black curls.

"May I help you?"

"My name is Isobel Watkins and this is my daughter Dory. We've come to thank you for the fine loaf of bread you sent."

Mrs. Jacobs rapidly blinking eyes betrayed her nervousness.

"I hope we haven't come at an inconvenient time," Ma said.

"No." Mrs. Jacobs seemed to relax a little. "How glad I am you are feeling better."

"Just about one hundred percent," Dory replied. Folks weren't exactly welcoming in this town, but Dory was confident their opinions of the Watkins would improve once they'd made Dory and Ma's acquaintance.

"I was just sitting down for some tea. Won't you join me?"

Ma said they would. Dory knew Ma hated coming empty-handed. Back in Kansas, paying a call meant bringing a jar of blackberry preserves or an apple cake fresh from the oven. They'd been able to show such hospitality along the trail but they were out of supplies for baking and the preserves they'd brought from home had been used up long ago.

Mrs. Jacobs asked them into the front room which was made up into a parlor. The two windows had curtains, frilly and white. A set of green chairs were padded with needlepoint covers. Dory could smell the woodsy scent of cedar.

Their hostess invited them to sit.

Ma took one of the green chairs and Dory took the other. They were nice to sit on. She was as comfortable as if they were back in the civilized world they'd come from.

Mrs. Jacobs excused herself and left the room. Dory hadn't expected Harley to be home but she was disappointed just the same not to see him here. A few minutes later his ma came back carrying a tray with a china teapot, cups and saucers, a pair of silver tongs and a pretty pink dish filled with sugar cubes. Dory eyed the sugar greedily.

"I'm afraid there's no cream," Mrs. Jacobs said. "Cows are in short supply here in Ragtown."

Her ma sat with her back straight and accepted the cup of tea with thanks. She picked up the silver tongs and added two lumps of sugar to her cup as if the sugar was no big deal.

Dory followed her example. The sugar cubes weren't white like back home but slightly gray with funny specks in them. Dory didn't care. Her mouth watered in anticipation of their sweet flavor.

Only after Mrs. Jacobs had settled into her chair and poured herself a cup of tea, did Ma take a sip from her cup. Dory did the same. The sweet flavor melted in her mouth, by far the best tea Dory had ever tasted.

"Harley told me about carrying you down to the river." Mrs. Jacobs stirred her cup with a silver teaspoon.

"Your boy was a big help," Ma responded.

"He's like that. Always trying to be a good citizen."

Ma nodded. "I don't ever recall ever being so under the weather. Luckily I have my daughter with me."

Both women smiled at Dory. She smiled back. She was becoming one of them, a lady who sat and drank tea with the ladies in the community.

"You have a lovely home," Ma said.

"Thank you," Mrs. Jacobs said. There was sadness in her voice.

"Have you lived in Ragtown long?" Ma asked.

"Almost two years now. My husband and a partner started a freighting business out of the Yuma territory. My Orville passed almost a year ago and me and my boy stayed on. Harley has a notion that he can pick up where his pa left off."

Ma's expression softened. No doubt she understood the hardship this woman faced without her husband. Hardship and loss seemed to dog just about everybody out west.

Dory's biggest fear had been her family would perish crossing the emigrant trail. They weren't out of danger yet.

Very soon they'd be headed into the mountains, one last and dangerous obstacle before they reached their destination.

Mrs. Jacobs put her cup and saucer down on a small table. "Ragtown is a harsh place. There's gambling, drinking and all kinds of carrying on. I'd advise your daughter to be careful when she's in town."

"Dory is a sensible girl," her ma said.

"As long as she keeps to her side of the road," Mrs. Jacobs replied.

"My side?" Dory asked. The woman talked as if Dory wasn't sitting right there across from her.

Mrs. Jacobs turned an indulgent gaze on Dory. "The main street of town is divided down the middle. The saloonkeeper and his people stay on their side. The cowhands and wranglers are not welcome to cross the line either. We coexist since neither knows how to get rid of the other."

"A convenient arrangement, I'm sure." Ma pursed her lips.

"There are those who cross out of necessity," Mrs. Jacobs went on. "Dr. McKinnon, for instance. He wouldn't refuse to set a broken bone or remove a bullet. The rest of us stay where we belong."

Dory understood the wisdom in the plan but wondered if the settlers put too much trust in that line. Seemed to her that a bullet didn't know which side of the road to stay on.

She didn't contradict their hostess, however. Dory knew her manners.

Besides, the gracious lady was the first female company she and her ma had enjoyed since Ma took ill and they'd been quarantined from the rest of their party.

She heard voices outside. The talk grew louder. Mrs.

Jacobs' frowned but she remained seated. She appeared to know who was arguing. Most likely, she knew why.

The door banged open and Harley marched in. When he saw the ladies he stopped abruptly and pulled off his hat. His face was red. His hair stuck out in every direction.

Dory stifled a giggle. He ran his hand over the top of his head which improved his look some. He was plainly agitated and full embarrassed in front of his ma and her company.

"I believe you've already met Mrs. Watkins and her daughter," his ma said.

Harley greeted Ma and turned to Dory. His gaze took in her clean dress and best bonnet, so different from the first time they'd met. He nodded at her with appreciation clearly evident and Dory was pleased he'd noticed.

"Morning, Dory. Good to see you," he said.

"We came to thank you for your help," Ma said.

"You're welcome," Harley said. He addressed his ma. "If you'll excuse me, I've chores to attend to."

Whatever Harley'd come into that house for had been set aside for another time., Dory decided. He turned and left them without a word of explanation.

"You've raised a fine boy," Ma said.

"Thank you," Mrs. Jacobs replied. "A difficult task given these surroundings."

Dory jumped up from her seat and set her cup and saucer down on the tray. "May I be excused? Harley looks like he needs somebody to talk to."

Both women agreed that her observation was a sound one.

Dory followed Harley outside. He'd crossed the front yard to a corral where several horses milled about. He'd hiked one booted foot to the first rail of the wooden fence and studied the stock with such attention most likely he didn't hear her approach.

"Are you all right?" she asked as she reached him.

He turned sharply, his body tense as a coil. When he saw who spoke, he exhaled. He was still mighty stoked up by whoever he'd been talking to over at the house.

"I couldn't help but hear you arguing just now," she said. "I'd like to help. I've been told I'm a very good listener."

Harley grasped the top rail of the fence. "One of these days, me and him will get into it. He's a mean *hombre* and I'm not going to let him push me around."

"Your pa's partner?" she asked.

"That's right. Ever since Dad died, he's been giving orders."

"Because you're young?" Dory asked.

Harley straightened. "I reckon that's part of it. I don't know why my dad joined up with him. The man's no good. He's rotten through and through and believe me when I tell you, the man has no soul."

Dory had known plenty of ornery people in her life. The boss of the wagon train, for instance. The man had little patience and even cussed at his horse. But a person with no soul she didn't understand.

Dory joined him at the fence. He was plenty worked up and needed to let off some steam. "Do you want to tell me what he said? Sometimes it's a good idea to share your troubles with a friend."

Harley took off his hat, scratched the top of his head and then put his hat back on. He looked mighty handsome in the morning light. She felt like she'd a belly full of fireflies.

"He wants me to fill up some barrels with water and

freight them out of the Forty Mile to sell to those trying to get across," Harley explained.

"Sounds like a fine business proposition to me," Dory replied. "Water's in short supply coming across the desert. I saw a lot of dead and dying livestock back there."

Harley shook his head. "He wants me to charge a big price for the water, as much as a dollar a barrel." Harley looked at the ground. "To my mind, that's taking advantage of folks in need."

Dory understood his point. Folk crossing the desert were desperate. That's what the Forty Mile did to people, made them desperate and easy prey.

"You could charge ten cents an animal and still make money since the water is free." She smiled. "I reckon those settlers would be grateful for not losing their stock to thirst."

Harley thought over what she'd said. "Sounds fair but my partner don't see it that way."

Dory appreciated he'd considered her idea and saw some merit to it.

The horses nickered and bobbed their heads. They were tall and stocky like Buck and Gussie and they were restless.

"All those horses belong to you?" she asked.

"Yup, they're my breeding stock."

"Where'd you come across such good-looking mares?"

"Did some trading with folks like your pa passing through."

"You're a good judge of horseflesh," she said.

"I like to think I'm a good judge of people too." There was conviction in his voice and a fair amount of self-importance. She didn't hold such notions against him. The territory wasn't a place for the timid.

"Let's take your stock down by the river. They can fill

their bellies with sweet grass." She gave him a flirtatious smile.

"Sounds like a good idea," he replied. He seemed to have gotten his temper under control.

They rounded up the mares and Harley set halters on them. She led a pretty dun-colored mare and he led the two others. When they reached the bank of the river, they staked the horses in a patch of wild grass.

The temperature was cooler down by the river. Harley's gaze followed the rushing water looking gloomy. She hadn't pegged him a thinking man but he brooded as they sat under a tree.

"I like your ma," she said, fumbling for words to take away his troubles.

"She's had a hard time since my dad died."

"She sure is proud of you. I can tell."

He raised his eyebrows in surprise. "Do you think so?"

"Know so."

He broke out in a grin.

Dory was tickled she'd been able to help with the change in his mood.

He leaned closer. He did have amazing eyes that showed kindness. "Would it be all right if I kissed you?"

Dory's heart beat wildly and she drew in a quick breath. She'd no experience with the rightness or wrongness of letting him kiss her. She only knew she wanted him to.

She closed her eyes and tilted her head upwards. His rough hands rested on her cheek bones.

"You smell so good," he said. "Sweet, like spring water."

She opened one eye. "Are you gonna kiss me or talk?"

Without further encouragement, he pressed his mouth

SARAH RICHMOND

on hers.

Heat rose in her face. The moment was exquisite in its simplicity. It was over too soon.

She took a deep breath and composed herself. It was foolishness letting Harley kiss her. Nothing could come of it and it'd be wrong to pretend otherwise.

When he leaned in for a second try, she prevented him with an outstretched hand. There was no doubt they liked each other but more important considerations prevented them from carrying on like this.

"Aw come on, Dory."

"I can't let you."

"Why not?"

"I think we ought to behave ourselves," she said, primly.

"It's only an itty, bitty kiss." He looked at her with that silly grin plastered on his face. He found her objections amusing, Dory could plainly see.

"Ma will be wondering where I am," she said, scrambling to her feet. She brushed off her dress and retied her bonnet.

He got up and stood over her like some big gawking bird. "You're a pretty little thing."

It was an awkward compliment but Dory accepted its sincerity. "Thank you."

"And I mean to court you," he said with confidence.

She needed to set him straight. "You listen to me, Harley Jacobs. You know courtin's an impossibility. Me and my ma are headed for California as soon as the next wagon train arrives. My pa depends on me. Just like you, I aim to do what's expected."

She left him to tend to his horses and climbed the rise to the path heading back to the Jacobs' place. She knew if she turned around he'd be watching her with that silly grin of his.

What they'd done was exciting and confusing. The kiss was more than she'd ever imagined a kiss could be. Her carnal urges blazed inside her like a prairie fire.

She hoped and prayed that Ma wouldn't guess what they'd been up to. Nice girls didn't even think about such things. Least ways, she was sure Ma had never had such thoughts.

He'd declared his intentions to court her. She'd let things go too far. She hoped he was enough of a gentleman to heed her wishes.

She'd made a promise to her pa and promises couldn't be broken.

To stave off further lapses in her good sense, Dory resolved not to see Mr. Harley Jacobs again.

# Chapter Four

MA WAS READY to leave the Jacobs' place when Dory returned. Dory tried to act normally but her mind was on that kiss. Ma didn't ask after Harley. Thankfully, she didn't seem to notice how Dory just about floated on air.

They said their goodbyes to Mrs. Jacobs. She asked them to come again and Ma said she would. The visit had renewed her spirits.

Walking though town, Dory tried to imagine the line Mrs. Jacobs talked about. Good thing she'd mentioned it, although Ma would've never walked anywhere near that saloon.

Dory chanced a glance at the other side of the street anyway. A girl about her age leaned out of one of the second story windows of the saloon. Her reddish hair was down on her shoulders. She wore nothing but a fancy corset and snowy white bloomers, revealing to the world what the good Lord had given her.

Dory looked away in alarm. Ma hadn't seen or if she did, she made no mention of the girl. Ma browsed the shop windows as they strolled along the boardwalk. Dory kept her mouth shut. She didn't want her ma to fret.

When the reached the last step, Dory looked behind her. The girl was gone.

They headed for the dirt road that would take them

back to their camp. Dory wondered who the girl was and why she'd ben staring at her and Ma.

When they reached their wagon, Ma sunk down into the kitchen chair, more worn out than she'd admit. Dory saw the suffering in her face, the pain that she tried to hide. The pain wasn't so much physical, like she broke her arm, but it was there all right, set deep inside and held by the conviction that all they believed and worked hard for would be shattered by something they couldn't name, by misfortune that knew no bounds.

Dory wondered if Ma would ever return to her old self. She wondered that about all of them. This land seemed to change those who came to tame her. Whether the change was good or bad, Dory couldn't say.

She removed her good bonnet and tied her flour sack apron around her waist. She thought about Harley and his brazen ways. His kiss had given her the shivers right down to her toes. Of course, a first kiss would leave an impression. She'd invited the kiss, to be sure, but he'd seemed ready and willing to carry on with more than one. He'd been so bold as to say he intended to court her.

Dory knew she had a lot to learn about such and all. She wished she could ask Ma about the first time Pa had kissed her. Ma wouldn't talk of such things and Dory missed her friends back home at a time like this.

One of these days Ma would sit down with her and explain what she needed to know about being a wife. First, they had to get to California.

Dory started out to collect brush for the fire. She thought about the saloon girl. What had brought her to Ragtown and why did she show herself in public in such a disgraceful way? Perhaps she didn't have a ma and pa who looked after her properly? Not like Dory whose separation from her pa was only temporary and whose family had been estranged by circumstances out of their control.

As Dory gathered up the dried-up tumbleweed, she resolved to stay away from that side of town. Her pa had warned her and pa wasn't given to idle conversation. He knew Dory's curious nature. Curiosity, he'd told her time and again, surely killed the cat.

She kept the image of her pa's soulful gaze and the sound of the boys' teasing laughter in her heart. She knew her ma did to, for when they said their prayers at night, Ma asked for special protection for Pa and her boys.

Dory supposed that was what a family was about. They took care of each other. She lifted her load and looked up into the big sky. She prayed right there and then that her family would be together again soon, reunited in that faraway place called California.

WORD CAME THAT a preacher passing through was holding Sunday service. Dory and her ma put on their good dresses and bonnets, determined to be among the faithful to worship.

As Dory looked in the square mirror she'd taken out of the trunk, she saw her sunburned face and freckles with dismay. She couldn't expect to keep a perfect complexion, not working under the hot sun that bore down on them day in and day out. She saw other changes as well. Her face had become thinner, making her eyes stand out in a face that was no longer a girl's. The bodice of her best dress revealed a womanly figure.

The tiny flower pattern was faded, worn out like the rest of them. She wished she had a piece of lace or ribbon to make the dress more attractive but she didn't and there wasn't time to make alterations anyway.

Ma called her and she put the mirror back in the trunk and shut the lid. One day soon she'd buy herself some calico cotton and sew herself a new dress. She stepped down from the wagon thinking about sewing up a matching bonnet. Wouldn't that look grand?

Ma sat in her chair, drinking out of a tin cup. Luckily the Carson flowed with cool, clean water. With September right around the corner, the rains would surely be coming.

Dory knew the importance of water. They'd gone without anything to drink in the last days of their crossing the desert. She'd passed the wretched bodies of livestock along the route that'd given out because of thirst. Harley's partner was just plain greedy asking a big price for water. Thank goodness Harley didn't have it in him to take advantage of folks.

This morning a breeze rustled through the vegetation along the river's banks. A peaceful sound, Dory decided as she tied the ribbons on her bonnet.

"We'd better be off," her ma said and she finished the remaining drops in her cup. Her bonnet framed her face in a way that made her look younger. When she smiled, all the seriousness of their situation seemed to melt away.

Ma stood and set the cup on the armrest of her chair. She was determined to go to the service and nothing Dory could've said would have persuaded her otherwise. The service was held outdoors near the cemetery. The land had been set aside for a meeting house that would be built one day. Today, they made do with what they had.

Most of the townsfolk were already gathered. Doc McKinnon and his wife nodded a greeting. The tall man who ran the mercantile stood beside a short, round woman and held the hand of a little girl. The girl, about ten years of age, wore pink ribbons in her hair. Her dress was made out of a pale pink silk. She looked like a doll Dory had once seen in the general merchandise store back home. That doll had porcelain skin and painted blue eyes and had been coveted by every girl in the county.

Harley and his ma were there. Despite the squawking jaybirds flapping inside her, she acted civilly when they greeted her.

He looked different with his hair combed and slicked back with store-bought oil. A thin mustache had sprouted on his upper lip. Lighter in color than his hair, it was barely visible. She might've not noticed except he kept touching his lip with his knuckles, a way of scratching politely in public.

He seemed pleased to see her until she noticed how he nodded at all of his neighbors with the same enthusiasm. Has she made too much of that kiss down by the river? Harley probably had a string of young ladies he kissed on a regular basis.

Looking around, she saw all kinds of folks gathered. Working men in jeans and buckskin, farmers in wool serge, gentlemen in black suits and string ties, ladies in calico and shiny silk taffeta and satin. This here was a community of people from every station in life. Some didn't even speak English so a person could understand but they'd all come together for a purpose.

Dory and her ma took their places among the crowd. From time to time, she glanced over and saw Harley staring at her. His mother didn't seem to pay him no mind nor the others who bowed their heads over their prayer books. When he caught her looking at him, he broke into one of his wide grins. She turned away and bit her lower lip, fighting a blush. She didn't want him getting the wrong idea.

She looked in the other direction. Away from the others, she caught a glimpse of a group of women dressed in starched petticoats, fine satin skirts and tailored jackets. Men looked sideways at them and the women ignored them.

Dory recognized the girl who'd leaned out of the window to gawk at her that day they'd visited Harley's ma. Her beautiful reddish-gold hair was gathered up on top of her head in fine ringlets. A fancy crimson and gold velvet hat sat perched on her head, secured with a hatpin encrusted in pearls. She looked neither left nor right but kept her gaze firmly planted on the preacher.

Dory reflected on how many of their practices had been altered since they started out from home. She wondered what Grandma Jerrold would say if she could see them in worship with saloon ladies. She could hear Granny's shrill voice, her index finger wagging in front of Dory's face, reminding her of how a lady never dressed in such a comely manner and how rouge and face powder were the devil's own devices.

Although Granny had been known to splash herself with a generous amount of toilet water bought with good money at the general merchandise store in town, Dory had heeded the old woman's counsel. She didn't see the harm in the many things her granny cautioned her about but she'd avoided the scolding Granny always seemed in a hurry to give.

The preacher was one of the fire and brimstone kind. He was tall with narrow shoulders and a sunken chest. He talked of Hell and how sinners were destined for its fiery eternity. Dory couldn't help but look back at the saloon women to see how they were taking this all in. Her mother cleared her throat and Dory swiftly turned back to the assembly.

They sang a song out of worn hymnals and Dory prayed that her pa and brothers had arrived safely in California. The prayer gave her some comfort, for she knew it was all she had at this juncture to protect her family. When the service was over, the preacher invited them to a reception in the Mercantile.

Ma agreed that they could go for a little while. Sunday was the Lord's Day and socializing should be kept to a minimum, but the separation from Pa and the boys was hard on them both and the company would be welcomed.

No such laxity in the rules would've taken place back in Ulysses. Rules were rules and were stridently obeyed.

When it came to the place where the imaginary line divided the town, nobody hesitated. The townsfolk headed for the mercantile and the saloon ladies turned toward the saloon. Cow pokes and wranglers who'd stayed away from the service waited on the boardwalk, talking loudly and joshing with each other. They followed the saloon women inside, their spurs ringing.

Dory couldn't exactly explain the fascination with those ladies. She supposed the Devil had a great deal to do with her curiosity about the saloon. A decent woman wouldn't set foot near those swinging doors but she'd hoped she could catch a peek of what was going on. When the doors swung back, Dory saw cowhands bunched up talking and drinking and a few tables and chairs where men played cards. She couldn't see the saloon lady who'd caught her attention.

"Come along, Dory," Ma said briskly.

Dory followed her ma into the mercantile. The room

was stuffy, the air full of grain dust. A punch bowl had been set out on a long table along with cakes made with white flour and set out on china plates. Her mouth watered for the tiny triangle-shaped confections plump with dried fruit.

The owner who'd shied away from them when they'd first arrived introduced himself as Mr. Miller. Then he introduced his wife and little girl whose name was Emma. Ma looked tickled pink to make their acquaintance and others came over and soon there was a crowd.

Dory greeted the residents of Ragtown, some newly arrived as she was and others who'd already set down roots. Emma ran off to the back of the store as soon as her ma gave her permission—a dutiful and polite child, Dory was gratified to see. Civilization as she'd known it had taken hold in Ragtown.

Ma and Mrs. Miller started to converse about the weather and the lack of rain. Mr. Miller excused himself and went to greet another couple who'd just come through the doorway.

Dory looked around the room.

Harley talked to a group of women, which included his ma. When he saw her, he left them and sauntered up to her as cocky as you please. He rubbed his upper lip with the back of his hands as if to draw attention to his mustache.

Dory had no intention of mentioning that she'd noticed.

"Hello, I haven't seen you around in a while," he said.

"I've been busy getting ready for leaving. The next wagon train should be through in a couple of weeks."

Harley's good-natured expression fell and Dory regretted her sharp tongue.

"I've been occupied myself," he said. "The freighting

business is doing well."

"I'm glad to hear it," she said with a reassuring smile.

His face lit up. Clearly, he wasn't the kind of man who took offense for long.

"Would you like something to drink?" he asked. "Mrs. Miller makes a tasty punch."

Dory nodded.

Mrs. Miller flitted around the punch bowl, dispensing the lemon-colored liquid in tiny cut glass cups.

"Your punch is the best I've ever tasted," Harley told their hostess.

"Thank you, kindly." Mrs. Miller beamed at the compliment. "I see you've met Dory."

"Yes, ma'am. Dory and I are becoming well acquainted."

Mrs. Miller raised her eyebrows. Dory'd taken her for a busybody right away. Now there'd be idle gossip told around the settlement about her and Harley.

"I reckon Harley makes himself known to just about everybody passing through Ragtown," Dory said.

Mrs. Miller wouldn't be put off the scent. She gave the two of them knowing glances as she gave Harley two full glasses.

Harley handed Dory one of them. He downed his punch in one gulp and returned the glass to the table before she'd taken a sip. Dory intended to take her time, being a lady and all.

She searched the crowd for her ma. Ma conversed with the preacher, a look of contentment on her face. Her color was almost back to normal and she stood straight and tall among the citizens of Ragtown. Dory was relieved that her ma seemed to be getting stronger but they shouldn't stay socializing too long.

Dory sipped her punch. The punch was sweet and refreshing.

Harley eyed the cakes and Mrs. Miller wasn't one to make a hungry man wait. She served both of them a plate.

Dory had never tasted a cake this good. Harley set to eating and finished without taking a breath. She couldn't help but laugh.

His gaze held hers. She knew she shouldn't encourage him so but he did make the day brighter.

The children went outside to spin hoops in the street. She wandered over to the window and Harley followed.

"Want to go down by the river?" Harley asked.

"No, thank you," Dory replied. She didn't want to repeat what went on the last time he'd taken her there.

Harley looked at her as if she was a piece of that cake. She felt self-conscious and patted her hair for any loose strand that might've fallen out of her bonnet. This simple gesture widened his smile. He stepped closer. She backed up into a barrel but didn't raise a fuss where Ma and everybody else could hear.

"We should stand outside on the boardwalk, there's no fresh air in here at all," she said. She walked passed him as prim as a schoolmarm.

Harley followed her out the door, placing his hand on the small of her back as if she needed steering. His gentle touch sent delicious chills up and down her spine but she dismissed them. She'd already made up her mind to resist Harley Jacobs' peculiar charm.

They stood in the shade of the new tin roof on the mercantile watching the children playing. He was very close, almost touching and she side-stepped away from him.

Harley's amorous mood shifted when a stranger came

riding up the street—a dapper-looking man wearing a black hat. His mustache, dark as night, had been waxed into two perfect curves. He offered Harley no greeting as he got off his horse and tied it to the hitching post.

"Is your mother inside?" the man asked.

Harley glared. He wasn't good at hiding his feelings, that was for certain. There was no love between the two men and Harley didn't pretend, even on the Lord's day.

Dory wasn't partial to Harley's hostile side and she saw no cause to be unsociable with the new arrival.

"Good morning," she said, friendly-like.

The stranger touched the brim of his hat as a way of replying and went into the mercantile.

"Who is he?" Dory asked but she'd already guessed. The man was the partner Harley had been arguing with the other day when she and Ma visited with Mrs. Jacobs.

"His name is Homer Lafferty. He was my dad's partner and now he's mine."

Harley started for the door but Dory stayed him with her hand. "There's no use bringing up hard feelings. Your ma wouldn't want an argument in front of the entire town."

Harley must've seen some wisdom in her words, because he stopped in his tracks. With a long look at the door he settled back against the rough-sawn wood of the hitching post.

Dory reached up and brushed a horsefly off his hat. He turned his full attention to her.

"Are you all right?" she asked.

"I don't know, Dory. Sometimes I get so angry with Dad dying like he did. We had big plans."

There was a world of hurt bound up in him and Dory would listen. In her experience telling made the grief easier.

"How did your pa die?" she asked.

His face bunched up in pure misery. The memory was still sharp as broken glass.

"The axle broke on a wagon he was driving from Santa Fe. He and a team of horses went over the side of a narrow stretch of road into a ravine. The fall broke his neck."

Dory rested a hand on his sleeve, wanting to comfort. She'd seen many an accident and its victims on the trail. Some were from carelessness but most were bad luck. Dory didn't know what she'd do without her pa and when she saw him again she'd give him the biggest hug, even though he'd most likely object.

Harley's loss would never be mended, she reckoned and what happened to his pa would always stay with him like a wound that wouldn't heal. She wished she could find a word that would soothe his troubled heart but she couldn't think of anything that would be enough.

A child squealed as his wheel spun over the imaginary line in the street, rolling toward the saloon. The other children looked in horror as they watched the wheel roll away and come to a stop against the side of the building. The youngster burst out crying.

Most of the children had kicked off their good shoes and rolled up their Sunday-best pant legs but none of them risked danger and a good switching by crossing the street to fetch that ring of iron.

Harley straightened, stepped off the boardwalk and strode across the dirt as pretty as you please. He picked up the hoop and started it rolling down the center of the road. The children ran after him, calling out and laughing as he tried his hand at keeping the wheel moving by pushing it with one hand.

The wheel fell over and one of the boys snatched it up.

Harley brushed his hands off on his pants. He looked back at her with a silly grin on his face.

He told the children to take their game out of the street and into a field past the smithy's shop. They heeded him and Harley watched them go. He picked up a little girl who had trouble keeping up with the others and carried her on his back to the mercantile.

"Found me a good 'un," he said.

The child wiggled and he let her down. She climbed the front steps. Dory opened the door so she could go inside.

Harley rested against the hitching post, his arms folded across his chest. He looked pleased with himself and she supposed that was to be expected. He'd done a good deed crossing the line in the middle of the road and fetching the children's hoop.

A man like him was a valuable asset to the community.

"I best be going," he said.

There was kindness in his gaze and playfulness. By all accounts she was still a girl but the feelings that made her tingly all over were a woman's.

She regretted their time together was over.

He set his hat back on his head and left her standing there. She'd seen the good in him but also a streak of hatred that ran deep. That man Lafferty left a burr under Harley's collar that was plain enough for anybody to see.

She'd noticed Mr. Lafferty hadn't come to their Sunday meeting, although she'd no call to hold his lapse in worship against him. She was beginning to trust Harley's judgment and he'd no doubt plenty of reasons for saying the man was no good. He'd even made the claim that the man had no soul.

Harley hated Mr. Lafferty and hatred wasn't a burden to be carrying around inside you.

One day soon they'd talk some more and maybe he'd tell her why.

She decided to head back inside when a flash of crimson distracted her. The girl she'd seen in the window and again this morning at the service was standing in front of the swinging door of the saloon. She looked at Dory with one hand on her hip and a dash of curiosity in her surly gaze. An elaborate feather dyed red to match her strawberry-colored hair dangled from the top of her head, replacing the hat she'd worn earlier. This time the saloon dolly smiled.

Dory felt her face flush with heat. There was a familiarity in the woman's gaze that she'd no right to show toward Dory.

Dory looked away. Without even as much as a howdy-do she turned around and proceeded into the mercantile.

HARLEY PAID THEM a visit that evening. The sun had already gone behind the tallest peaks of the purple mountains. The dust had settled and the air had turned cooler, reminding them that winter was right around the corner.

He wore the lavender kerchief, freshly washed and ironed. He carried a bunch of yellow sagebrush flowers, a man who'd come a courting.

Dory and her ma exchanged glances.

"You'd better put a fresh pot of coffee on," Ma said.

Dory rose from her seat. There was no hiding Harley's intentions from Ma now. He walked with an easy stride as he came down the gentle slope to their camp. She had some prideful thoughts when he reached her.

"Hello, Dory." He held out the cluster of sage for her to take.

The tiny pale flowers smelled of the familiar scent of woods and wilderness. They weren't the prettiest flowers she'd ever seen but she was touched by what he'd done.

"Why, thank you," she said, sniffing them as if their summertime fragrance was the rarest of perfumes.

"I know they're not what you're used to."

Dory didn't let on that she'd never had a gentleman caller bring her flowers before.

"Maybe so but I like them just the same," she said.

He looked mighty handsome standing in the firelight. Harley greeted Ma and snatched off his hat.

"Come join us, will you?" Ma asked. "Dory was just putting on a fresh pot of coffee."

"Thank you, ma'am. I will sit a spell."

"I'm worn out, you take my chair." Ma rose and drew her shawl tighter. "I was about to go to bed. Morning will be here before you know it."

Harley waited until Ma disappeared into the wagon and then slumped down on the kitchen chair. Dory ladled water into the coffee pot from the rain barrel that she'd filled from the river while there was still light. She added some chicory and set the full pot on one of the rocks near the smoldering fire. Then she added water to one of the tin cups and arranged the flowers in it. She replaced the lid on the barrel and put the flowers on top. Their smell was a delight.

Before Harley'd arrived, Dory had been pondering about that saloon dolly and her forward ways. She'd been wondering about all she'd heard about women of that sort and the other names they were called. Time she set those thoughts aside.

"Nice service," she said, taking a seat on the opposite side of the fire. It seemed a good idea to keep a distance between them.

"Yup."

"That preacher come around here often?"

"Maybe once a month. He tends to a big flock." Harley grinned.

Dory shook her head. Grinning just seemed to come natural to the man.

"Seems to me the town could use a full-time preacher," she said.

He leaned forward. The light from the fire flickered across his face. "We'll have one day. We'll build a church. And a schoolhouse. Heck, we'll even hire a sheriff. The town won't be a roughneck settlement. Ragtown will be downright respectable."

"Now Harley Jacobs, how can a town be respectable?" she asked, laughing.

He colored up a bit. "You know what I mean."

She knew exactly what he meant. He intended to build Ragtown into a place of permanence. She looked up at the town, silhouetted against the sky. Ragtown looked like a strong wind would blow it clear to the mountains.

She realized Harley was a dreamer. She didn't hold it against him. A man had to have a dream, she reckoned, a plan to leave this life better then he found it. Why did Harley have to pick this place?

"I hope we live near a town in California. Pa wants to pan for gold but I'd go plumb crazy if I didn't have anybody my own age to talk to."

Harley's smile faded. "Did you ever think about staying here?"

"In this sorry excuse for a town?" She scoffed.

"There's nothing more to this town than rickety old tents."

"It's not so bad." His gaze was forceful. He had something on his mind and Dory knew where the conversation was headed. She'd better set him straight here and now about what the future held for her.

"Ragtown isn't for me," she said kindly for she'd no wish to hurt him.

"Why the heck not?" He looked surprised. "The Nevada territory is as good as anywhere to set down roots."

Regrettably, she'd put him on the defensive. She didn't want to argue but he had to know where she stood.

"First ways," she said patiently, "there isn't much more to this town than patches of dried-up grass and sagebrush."

"You could put in a garden. All kinds of good things would grow."

"Maybe," she replied. "But what about trees? There aren't any trees except for the cottonwoods down here by the river. Even they don't pass for trees, all bent and twisted as they are, and they don't give much shade."

He opened his mouth but she kept going. "Even if trees did grow, it'd take a number of years before they could be useful."

She'd stumped him on that one.

"It won't be easy," he replied after some reflection. "We're going to make this the kind of town folks will be proud of."

"I'm headed for California," she said firmly. "There's everything I need across those mountains. Pa calls it the land of milk and honey."

Harley had nothing to add and she was grateful. She didn't like arguing with him. He was just as firm in his opinion as she was. Nothing was going to change either of their minds.

They listened to the sounds of the night, the call of a faraway bird and the fire crackling.

He pulled off his hat. His hair was still slicked down by the hair oil he'd rubbed in it this morning. He'd looked like a proper gentleman, or as close as a man could get living out here in the middle of nowhere.

"Dory, I'm rare fond of you."

Ever mindful her mother was only a few yards away, Dory hushed him up. "Don't speak so."

The coffee began to boil over. She jumped up and pushed it back from the heat.

"I'd like you to stay," he said with the arrogance of a man.

Dory turned to face him. "How could you ask such a thing after I've explained myself in plain English that I'm going west."

He seemed unfazed by her outburst and gazed at her, grinning like a polecat. "I've got a thousand acres of good ranch land not far from here. I'm gonna build a fine frame house with a front porch facing the mountains. It'll be a lot of hard work, but I'm strong."

"You stop right there," she cried. Tears welled in her eyes, tears that shouldn't be there.

Harley looked at her with such gentleness her heart was fit to break. The conversation had put her in a state. Her mind was befuddled with the mixed emotions that raged inside her. He'd no right to include her in his dreams. No right at all.

"Time you left," she said.

Harley stood and put on his hat. "Promise me you'll think on my offer."

"I will but I don't know what good it'll do."

He strode off, a man who'd asked an important question. She waited until he'd disappeared before she went to the wagon. Her ma surely would've heard what Harley had said and she didn't want her ma to worry.

"Ma, are you asleep?" Dory peeked inside.

Ma sat on her bed brushing out her hair in the dark.

"Harley left so soon?"

Dory climbed inside. "We quarreled."

"About what?"

"He asked me to stay in Ragtown."

Ma stopped brushing. "What did you tell him?"

"What could I say? I didn't mean to lead him on. I surely didn't." She wanted Ma to explain the turmoil that brewed inside her, the ache that wouldn't go away.

"Of course, you didn't."

"He took a giant leap from flirting to courting and now this."

"A man needs an answer one way or the other."

"I gave him my answer but he wouldn't have it." Dory sat down and rested her head in her ma's lap. Ma began stroking her hair as she'd done many times when Dory was a child.

"He must believe there's a chance."

"Ma, I can't leave you. I promised Pa I'd get you to California. I'm not going to break my promise."

"I know."

Dory could hear Ma's breathing. The touch of her hand was a comfort. Her ma needed her. She'd never forgive herself if she let her ma and pa down.

"I'll find Harley come morning and make him listen," she said. "When I explain I've made my mind up, he won't pester me anymore."

THE NEXT MORNING, Dory went to Harley's house directly after she'd finished her chores. His mother was washing up dishes in a tin tub behind the house. Mr. Lafferty was there. Whether he'd come over for business or a friendly visit, Dory couldn't say. Harley's ma seemed to pay Mr. Lafferty little mind. She looked relieved when Dory announced herself.

Mr. Lafferty touched the brim of his hat and said hello. He did seem like a very polite fella. Too bad he'd gotten on the worst side of Harley's otherwise easygoing nature.

"I'm sorry but Harley's gone, Dory. He left first thing," his ma replied to her inquiry. "Said he has something important to do.

Dory was surprised. He hadn't mentioned a trip last night. Given the topic of their discussion and all, most likely telling her about the trip had gone out of his head.

"Where did he go?" she asked.

"He went toward the mountains," his ma answered. "He went to California."

"He should've been on his way to Santa Fe. There's a load of supplies needs hauling," Mr. Lafferty said.

Mrs. Jacobs frowned. Dory too, didn't like Mr. Lafferty suggesting Harley shirked his duties in their freighting business.

She thanked Harley's ma and left them to their conversation.

Of course, Dory was disappointed Harley had taken off but maybe this sudden departure was for the best. The separation would make living in Ragtown easier as she waited for the next wagon train to arrive. She hated to think their quarrel had anything to do with his leaving and she hoped he would be back before they left so she could say a proper goodbye.

She was thinking these thoughts as she strolled down the dusty street. A buckboard filled with dry goods was being unloaded at the Miller's mercantile by a fella with a long beard. A pair of sad-faced mules hung their heads.

Tin-panny music drifted from the saloon. As Dory passed, the saloon dolly who'd been watching her appeared in the doorway. She rested a lily-white hand on the curved top of the door, looking at Dory.

Dory stared back. What she saw surprised her. The saloon dolly wasn't a woman at all but a girl. The girl's pretty face was marred by rouge and powder. Her lips were as red as fire.

This time Dory's irritation with the girl riled her enough to speak out. "What are you looking at?"

The girl glanced behind her as if Dory had spoken to somebody else. She looked back at Dory, uncertain.

So Dory headed for the imaginary line to give this girl a piece of her mind about good manners.

# Chapter Five

"**I** NEED YOUR help," the girl said. She pushed through the swinging doors and met Dory half way.

Dory parked her hands on her hips, not sure this was one of her best ideas. She was thoroughly flabbergasted because there was no way she could help the likes of somebody who spent their time in a saloon.

"What are you talking about?" Dory shot back. "What kind of help do you want from me?"

The girl looked around her like she was scared. "Not here. Not where the others can hear us."

Dory huffed. They stood in the middle of the road in broad daylight. There'd be no keeping their meeting a secret.

"Please," the girl said, pleading.

Where in the world did the girl expect Dory to go with her? She'd already done a bad thing by talking to her. Crossing the line would be out of the question.

Not even the heavy paint all over the girl's face could disguise her fear. Dory couldn't refuse.

"Meet me behind the livery," Dory said.

The girl nodded and swung around. The fancy dress rustled like leaves in a summer breeze. She walked back to the saloon with dignity, a quality Dory wouldn't have thought to be in a saloon dolly's character.

Dory stepped up onto the boardwalk and walked in the

direction of the livery. The man unloading the buckboard
had just about emptied the back of his wagon. She saw
through the window Mr. Miller helping a customer who
was buying a sack of two-penny nails. When he saw her
passing by, he waved. She waved back. He was a lot
friendlier than when they'd first arrived and the sickness
had made him shy away from her and Ma.

She came to the end of the walkway and wondered if
this wasn't a mistake, meeting a painted lady. What could
she possibly want from Dory? Having given her word,
Dory wouldn't back out, and something in the girl's
anxious look drove Dory to find out what the girl wanted.

She stepped off the last board and headed for the worn-
out tent where the town blacksmith had set up his shop.
Clouds of black smoke rose in a column from the other
side of the tent. A team of horses was tied up to a hitching
post. She heard the steady rhythm of the forge, the clinking
of metal on metal, the whoosh of bellows and the crackling
of the fire as the smithy heated a piece of iron and pounded out a new shoe.

Dory didn't see the saloon girl at first. The back of the
smithy's tent was littered with barrels and wooden boxes.
A broken plow lay on its side. She trod carefully over the
scattered odds and ends until the woman appeared from
behind one of the stack of boxes. She was wringing her
hands. She had something powerful to tell Dory. Something Dory could help her with. Something she wished to
hide from the rest of the settlement.

"What's this all about?" Dory asked.

The girl went pale underneath all her rouge and powder.

"Thank you, Dory, thank you for coming," she spoke
in a soft voice.

"How do you know my name," Dory snapped.

"I've heard it spoken in the street. I heard your ma say it. Your ma is a lovely woman."

"Why are you spying on me and my ma?"

The girl grabbed Dory's hand. Her flesh was cold but soft like flower petals. She smelled as sweet as new grass.

Dory pulled back but she brought Dory's hand to her belly.

"I'm going to have a baby," the girl declared.

Dory felt the rounded form covered by the folds of the fancy dress. Her mind registered disbelief. She'd heard of women making babies without a husband. Such a disgrace had happened back home but she'd never known anyone personally who'd brought such shame to herself and her family.

Dory withdrew her hand. The girl looked at her with desperation and hope. Dory didn't have it in her to be critical of the girl.

"What is your name?" Dory asked gently.

"Adele Brewster."

"Where are your folks?"

Adele's expression shifted to one of pure unhappiness. "I don't have none. I was raised in an orphanage back in St. Louis."

Dory was beginning to understand and she made up her mind to give what help she could to Adele. No one should be alone, especially under these circumstances.

"There's a doc in this town. His name's Dr. McKinnon. He helped my ma when she had the sickness. He's the best one to get you through this."

"I know of him. I couldn't go to him by myself."

"You have to," Dory said firmly. "A baby is a serious matter and you should see him at once."

Adele gazed at the ground. "I'm afraid to go by my-self."

"Afraid of the doc?"

Adele lifted her gaze. "I can't go to his place. His wife will scorn me and I'll be turned away."

Dory hadn't forgotten Mrs. McKinnon's coldness when she'd sought help for her ma.

Adele looked like she was at the end of her tether. She needed help. Just as important, she needed a friend.

Dory had an idea. "I'll bring the doc here. You rest in the shade of this tent." She set a box on its end. "Take a load off. I won't be long."

Adele sat down on the box. She pulled a lacy handkerchief from under her sleeve and dried up her tears. Dory couldn't help but notice how delicate and ladylike Adele's hand was with fine-boned fingers and clean fingernails.

Dory didn't stay a moment longer. As she hurried, she thought about going to get Ma since her ma was closer. Ma would know what to do. She'd told Adele she'd fetch the doctor so that's where she headed.

She arrived at the edge of the boardwalk and climbed the steps. A pair of ladies passed her, nodding agreeably. Dory acknowledged their greeting with a quick hello. There was no time for polite conversation. She wasn't about to tell them where she was going.

When she reached the doc's house, she was out of breath. She rapped on the door.

Dr. McKinnon opened it. Dory was relieved that he was home.

He wore dark trousers held up by braces. He clutched a newspaper in his hand.

"I need you to come right away," she said, stammering as she struggled for breath.

"Is it your mother?" he asked.

"No, somebody who needs you bad. She can't come here."

The doctor didn't need any more convincing. He shrugged into his coat and grabbed his bag off a chair in the hallway. He called out to his wife that he was going out. He took his hat off a hook and squashed it on his head.

Mrs. McKinnon came to the door, wiping her hands on a kitchen towel. "Hello, Dory, I hope everything is all right at the camp."

"Right as can be," Dory replied.

"Has somebody else come down with the sickness?" she asked in a frightened voice.

"No, ma'am."

Mrs. McKinnon looked at her husband, her face drawn up in a pucker.

"There's nothing to worry about, Mary," Dr. McKinnon said.

His wife didn't look reassured. She wrung her hands out on that kitchen towel.

"I'll keep your coffee warm," she said.

Dr. McKinnon patted her arm affectionately and then motioned for Dory to lead the way.

Dory matched the doc's stride. He was a serious man and skilled at doctoring. She respected him but couldn't help but wonder how the McKinnons found their way to Ragtown.

People gave them funny looks as they reached the boardwalk. Doc carried his bag and folks stopped anyway to say hello. Doc greeted them by name but he didn't break his stride.

Mrs. Miller poked her head out of the mercantile.

"Good morning," she said in a high-pitched voice. "Where you off to in such a hurry?"

Dr. McKinnon stopped and shucked his hat and then planted it firmly back on his head.

Dory's heart sank. This was no time to be sociable.

"Good morning, Ruth. I've got a patient to attend to."

"Not your dear mother?" Mrs. Miller asked Dory.

"No, ma'am."

Mrs. Miller turned to Dr. McKinnon for more information.

Thankfully, the doc didn't dawdle. "Can't explain right now, Ruth. You understand."

Mrs. Miller shot Dory a curious look but said no more.

When they reached the end of the boardwalk, Dr. McKinnon was red-faced and breathing hard. "How much longer, Dory?"

"Not far. Over yonder by the smithy's tent."

She led him to where she'd left Adele. When they arrived, Adele stood up so quickly she knocked over the box she'd been sitting on.

Dr. McKinnon seemed to know right away what the problem was. He righted the box and told Adele to sit down. He put his bag on the ground and opened it. Dory tried to take a look at what he kept in his kit. She hadn't been in the frame of mind for looking when the doc came to tend to Ma. Now she peered inside this magic bag and saw the collection of metal instruments and bottled potions.

Dr. McKinnon disentangled a long stethoscope and poked the end pieces in his ears.

Adele looked at Dory with gratitude. Dory smiled to help the girl get over her big case of nerves. The examination only took a few minutes. He listened to her heart just as the doc had done back home to Dory and the boys. He looked at Adele's eyes and pulled down her eyelids. He felt the mound that was a baby growing.

"The pains have started," Adele told him.

"How long have you had them?" Doc asked.

"A day or so."

Doc folded his stethoscope and dropped it into his kit. "I'm going to look at your privates."

Adele picked up her skirt and her layers of fancy petticoats. Dory turned her back, deciding Adele would want her to.

"Good. I don't see any evidence of disease," Doc said.

Dory heard the snap of his bag and she turned around tentatively.

Adele straightened her skirt and didn't seem at all embarrassed about what the doc had done.

"Will she be all right?" Dory asked.

"As far as I can tell, although she's not had proper nutrition." He addressed Adele. "You should have come to me earlier."

Adele teared up. "I didn't know if I could. I mean, I didn't know if you'd see me."

Doc made a sound of disapproval in his throat as he picked up his bag. "We don't have much time. Ragtown is going to have a new citizen."

Adele looked frightened. Her fear brought on tender feelings in Dory.

She put her arm around Adele. "Don't you fret."

"You need fresh milk," Doc McKinnon said sternly.

Milk, Dory knew full well, was precious rare in the territory.

"I have some pills," Doc opened his case again and took out a brown bottle. "They're for anemia. Take one of these each morning."

Adele took the bottle and clutched it to her bosom.

"I must insist," Doc continued in his serious voice. "No alcohol and no intercourse."

Now Dory knew what the doc spoke of but she'd never heard anybody say the word out loud when referring to the act of copulation. The doc was a man of science and there was no cause for her to be ill at ease. Even so she fought a blush that burned from her neck all the way up to the top of her head.

Living on a farm, Dory knew how animals made babies. When Pa'd brought over the Simpson's prize bull in the spring, they'd all known the whys and wherefores of how calves came to be born.

It didn't seem possible that Adele could've done such a deed with somebody who wasn't her lawfully wedded husband. In the eyes of God, what she'd done was a sin.

Dory would be a married lady, of course, when she had her babies. The instruction on what to do would take place on her wedding day and only from her ma. Adele had no one to tell her these things, coming from an orphanage.

"I have no place to go," Adele said, almost in a whisper, "except back to the saloon."

Doc McKinnon rested his big hand on Adele's shoulder. "You can't go back there. You'll be putting your baby in harm's way if you do."

He turned to Dory. "You did good bringing me here. This baby will be here before we know it."

"How soon?" Adele whimpered.

"These things are never exact. Your pains are false labor, but I'm reasonably sure your baby will be with us before the week is out."

"Thank you, Doctor." Adele took a gold piece out from the bodice of her dress and handed it over to the man.

Doc shook his head. "You keep that money for your youngster."

Adele's face puckered and her lower lip trembled.

"I leave you in good hands," he told Adele. "Dory, you come fetch me if there's any change."

He left Dory standing there slack-jawed. The doc just gave her a responsibility she didn't want. She'd assumed he would take Adele over to his house. With his wife so flighty, maybe that wasn't such a good idea.

Dory watched him head for home. Her confused state of mind wasn't lost on Adele.

"Thank you, Dory, for all you've done. Don't you worry none, I'll manage. I've been on my own for a lot of years. I can take care of myself."

Dory whirled around. "Don't talk nonsense. Birthing a baby isn't something you can do by your lonesome. At a time like this, you need friends and family around you."

"The girls in the saloon are my friends," she said bravely as she tucked the gold piece back where it'd be safe.

Dory knew this was a lie. She hadn't gone to any one of those women, nor the man who owned the saloon, for help.

Dory didn't shame the girl by reminding her of this fact.

"What do they know about birthin' a young'un?" Dory said instead.

Adele covered her face with a trembling hand. Her body shook as she wept.

Dory hadn't meant to speak harshly. Adele carried on as if her heart was broken. The truth was Adele had no one in this world to see her through this and Dory put her arm around the girl's quaking shoulders and told her to hush, that everything was going to work out. They just had to put their heads together and figure what they needed to do.

Before long, Adele stopped her crying and blew her nose.

"My best idea is to take you to our camp," Dory said. "Ma won't mind when I tell her what you're up against."

"Your ma won't worry that I'm not respectable?" Adele sniffed.

"Oh, she'll mind and she'll consider you a fitting candidate for some bible learning but she won't turn you away. Not a girl in your condition."

"Oh, Dory, I knew you'd help me." Adele pushed herself up from her seat on the barrel. She wrapped her arms around Dory's neck and hugged her tightly.

"Now don't overdo it," Dory said, but she was pleased she could be a friend to someone who surely needed a friend.

AS PREDICTED, MA took Adele in. She didn't speak about what Adele had done to get herself in a family way.

Adele had it in her mind to do her share of the chores but Ma wouldn't hear such nonsense. She waited on the saloon lady like she was a princess come to visit. The bulk of the work fell to Dory.

When it was time to turn in, Adele stripped off her fancy gown. Dirty pink ribbons held up her stockings. Those stockings had holes run clean through them. Ma never wasted anything that had some use left but she threw the stockings and garters into the fire.

Ma gave Adele one of Dory's cotton nightgowns to wear, the one Dory'd been saving until they reached their new home. Ma gave up her bed in the wagon. Adele protested but Ma took her by the shoulders and looked at her woman to woman.

"Now I'm not your ma but you're going to do what I say," she said. "You'll do that baby no good sleeping on the ground."

"Yes, ma'am," Adele replied as meek as a mouse. She did what Ma asked.

Ma bedded down with Dory underneath the wagon. Dory snuggled in her blanket, wondering what it'd be like growing up without a ma and pa. Harley lost his pa and most likely would carry his loss 'til the day he died.

That night she missed her pa more than ever.

THE NEXT MORNING, Ma was up before dawn building up the fire for breakfast. Dory lingered under her blanket, listening to the awakening sounds of the many birds who lived along the river. She wondered where Harley had gone and when he'd be back. She'd spoken strong words to him but that'd been necessary so he wouldn't get any wrong ideas about her staying in Ragtown. She wished he'd come back.

The wagon creaked and Dory heard Adele moving about overhead. There'd be talk in town about her and Ma taking in Adele. More than likely, the ladies would shun them for what they'd done. Dory was proud that her ma had shown compassion for a frightened girl who needed help.

Adele climbed out the back of the wagon with her bloomers showing. She didn't show much modesty, a sin according to Grandma Jerrold. Dory reckoned Adele had a lot to learn about becoming a mother.

Dory shucked off her blanket reluctantly. She'd wanted to think about Harley some more, ponder on what she'd say to him when he got back, but there was work to be done.

Ma sat in the kitchen chair by the fire, letting the waist out of Dory's favorite cotton dress. Adele had gone off yonder to relieve herself.

"She's just a child," Ma said, stabbing the cloth with her needle.

Dory looked at that dress with dismay. There'd be no arguing with her ma. Adele needed proper clothes and the dress Dory had on still had plenty of wear left.

"She and I are about the same age," Dory replied.

"Yes, well…"

Dory poured herself a cup of coffee and sat down on a flat rock. "How old were you when you and Pa got hitched?"

Ma looked up, her gaze sharp. "I was all of eighteen and we had my father's permission."

"I'm nearly eighteen," Dory said. "I expect it's not far off now that I'll have a family of my own."

"You've plenty of time," Ma said. She didn't smile.

"I know but I think about such things…"

"With your pa gone, I don't know what I'd do if you decided to marry."

This was the first Ma spoke her opinion of Harley's offer. She'd known when he'd brought the flowers but held her tongue. When Dory had confided that Harley had asked her to stay, Ma had only replied that a man needed answering one way or the other.

Having Adele here had brought up Ma's protective nature and now she was in a fearsome worry.

Dory couldn't let her ma work herself into a state.

"There's nothing to fret about," Dory said, reassuringly. "I don't intend to go against what you and Pa want."

Her ma continued her sewing. "You must stay away from the saloon. It's a dangerous place."

Dory realized there was more than her flirtation with Harley that worried her ma. Having Adele with them reminded Ma that Dory was vulnerable to men who frequented the wrong side of the road. Her pa being gone and all, they'd no one to protect them.

"I will, Ma," Dory answered in earnest. "No harm's gonna come to me."

Ma looked up and this time she smiled. "All right, Dory. I see you've given this some thought and you won't do anything foolish."

Dory stood and kissed her ma on the cheek, strengthened by the confidence her ma showed in her.

"Off with you," her ma said. "We need fuel to keep this fire going."

The words that needed to be spoken had been said and agreed upon. It was the first adult conversation she'd had with her ma. She hoped their conversations would get easier.

Dory wasn't one to dwell on those things that made for discomfort. She finished washing up and went off to find tinder for the fire. As she picked up dried out bundles of brush, she decided they'd all be better off when this awful town was behind them.

# Chapter Six

D ORY'S NEXT JOB of the morning was to find fresh milk for Adele. There weren't any dairy cows in these parts to speak of but Ma heard from Mrs. Miller about a Mexican family who raised goats at their homestead. Goat's milk was as good as any cow's milk, Dory decided. Ma agreed.

As far as Dory knew, Harley hadn't returned from his trip across the mountains. Dory spent too much time thinking about Harley Jacobs. It was best to put him out of her thoughts.

Except she'd kissed him down by the river that day when she and Ma had gone calling on Mrs. Jacobs. That kiss had been the finest moment of her life. There was no denying it and she'd never forget it.

Adele saw Dory with the tin jug. She guessed her purpose. "Where will you find milk?"

"There's a ranch over in the foothills."

"Milk will cost you money."

Dory'd hoped to appeal to the rancher's charitable side for a soon-to-be new mother.

Adele pulled out the gold piece and pressed the heavy coin into Dory's hand. "Take this for payment."

Dory looked at her ma.

"That much money will buy a lot of milk," she said.

Ma hadn't thought payment would be necessary either

but this place was different from back home. Kindness wasn't a currency. Adele knew that better than the Watkins clan did.

Dory tucked the coin into the band of her bonnet.

Ma bid Adele to come and sit by her. Adele did as she was told. The two chatted amiably. Dory tried not to be bothered by their carrying on like two hens, but she wished she could stay and join them.

Bolstered by purpose and a sense of responsibility that Dory wouldn't shirk from, she headed in the direction of the mountains.

THE ROAD TO the ranch wasn't much more than a cart path. The ruts weren't as deep as the trail they'd come across on the Forty Mile but the worn stretch of road was certainly a sign of civilization going somewhere.

Dory walked in a part of the territory that a body shouldn't go without carrying a weapon. Snakes and lizards were always a threat, as were the lions who came out of the rocky foothills to prey on jackrabbits and other small critters. The big cats were the color of the soil she'd been told, sandy brown and difficult to spot but they were out there all right. She began to grow fearful that she should've brought Pa's shotgun. She picked up a good size rock. A rock would have to do if she came across one of those lions looking for an easy meal.

Parts of the path were flat but sometimes the road took climbing. The sun bore down with its relentless heat. The tin canister she carried grew heavier. She wasn't even sure she'd come the right way as she looked down at the valley below, at the place called Ragtown looking like it'd sprouted up out of a cloud of dust.

She settled against a stone ledge and rested. The view all around her about took her breath away. The peaks and valleys of the Sierra Nevada mountains spread out along the horizon. Somewhere out there her pa and the boys had crossed into California. Harley had taken the same route, no doubt, for his freighting business. In only a week or so, she and Ma would make their way across this rugged land. The view reminded her of how far she'd come and how far she'd yet to go. She felt alone up here by herself, a bit of a girl pretending to be a woman.

Dory wiped off her brow with the back of her hand. There wasn't any more time to waste. She picked up the tin jug and the rock and started off. She didn't have far to go. Over the next ridge, the ranch appeared as if it was a mirage. A stone and mud house stood out against the backdrop of a line of mountain peaks. A corral held a burro. A lean-to served as a barn.

She quickened her step. The homestead was neat and clean with chickens clucking in the yard. A woman carrying a child came out of the door of the house.

"I've come for milk," Dory said, hoping the woman spoke English. "Have you any to spare?"

The woman's gaze went to the tin and then to the rock.

"In case I come across a lion," Dory explained and she set the rock on the ground.

Clearly satisfied Dory meant her no harm, the woman gestured for Dory to follow her. They walked across the yard and behind the lean-to where a man dug a post hole. Another child helped. He stopped when he saw Dory. The woman spoke rapidly to him in a language Dory took to be Spanish.

The man greeted Dory with a hello. His teeth were

heavily stained but his smile was friendly. Thankfully, he spoke some English. She listened closely as he spoke rapidly. She picked out some of the words, understanding he would sell her some milk.

Dory reached up on her bonnet and removed the gold piece. "I have payment."

She held out the coin.

The woman's eyes widened.

"*Gracias*," the man said.

Dory pressed the gold into the woman's hand.

"*Gracias*," she repeated, giving Dory a grateful smile. The man motioned for Dory to come with him.

The goats were in a pen made from brush piled high and reinforced with sticks. The pen was a good one and would keep the goats from wandering. No lion would be discouraged by three feet of thicket which explained the musket. which stood upright against the outside of the pen, ready for use if need be.

The stink brought flies. Dory didn't mind the smell. She was used to such smells from their farm back home, but the flies just about drove her to distraction. She shooed them away by waving her hands but those pesky flies kept on biting.

The farmer climbed inside the enclosure. The goats bawled and begged to be let out. They'd like to eat some of the tender mountain grass, Dory reckoned, although she'd heard that a goat will eat just about anything and not complain.

The farmer tied up a she-goat and felt her bag. Whether she'd been milked this morning, Dory couldn't tell. The man carried a three-legged stool over from one corner of the pen and sat down.

Dory was glad to have fresh milk straight from the

source. Adele and her baby would surely benefit.

He filled the tin jug and replaced the lid. He lifted the jug over the hedge to Dory. It was heavier than she'd imagined but she thanked him using the word they'd spoken to her. She carried the jug by its handle using both hands. The woman waited in the shade of her house. Her youngster clung to her skirt.

Dory thanked her for her help.

She picked up the rock and held it out to Dory. Dory shook her head. She'd no way to carry it. She'd have to make the journey back to camp without a rock to protect her.

The woman bid her farewells in a foreign tongue.

Dory started over the rocks and up the path, the bulk of the milk jug making her steps awkward. Soon she was at the place where the sheer cliff revealed the town below. This time instead of admiring the view, she thought of how far she still had to go lugging her load.

She descended the steep grade slowly. Carrying the jug made navigating difficult. One slip of her foot in the gravel and she could easily fall.

A lizard scurried off a rock, startling her. When she saw the ugly creature, she couldn't help but laugh.

"You're as scared of me as much as I am of you, I reckon."

The critter moved his head up and down as if in agreement.

She pressed on, knowing that Ma and Adele waited on her.

Dory stopped to catch her breath more times than she could count. Her arms and shoulders ached and the front of her dress was soaked with perspiration. She struggled with the jug which seemed to grow heavier with each step.

The path widened. She was almost to the road. From her perch, she saw a man in a buckboard coming her way. Her heart leapt with joy until she realized the man was Mr. Lafferty.

With as much effort as she could muster, she lifted the jug over the last outcropping of jagged rocks. He pulled up his team. A ride back to town would be a luxury but she dare not accept an offer. Harley said the man couldn't be trusted and Dory respected Harley's estimation of the man.

"Howdy, Miss Dory," Mr. Lafferty said, touching the brim of his hat.

Dory rested the jug on the ground between her feet. The hot sun overhead brought more perspiration running down her forehead. She wiped at her face with her sleeve, embarrassed for him to see her in such a state.

"Morning, Mr. Lafferty. You're a ways from town."

"I heard you were headed out this way. I thought you'd need a helping hand."

She wondered who'd told him about her.

"Has Harley returned?" she asked.

"No, not yet."

"Where did he go?"

"He didn't tell me." Mr. Lafferty adjusted his hat. "He's been real quiet since his pa died. A boy like that takes his pain inside and don't give himself any time to heal."

Dory thought Mr. Lafferty was more insightful than Harley gave him credit for.

"His loss is deeper than anybody knows," she said.

Mr. Lafferty nodded. "Put your load in the back and come on up. We'll be back in town in no time."

He was being neighborly and Dory reconsidered accepting the offer to help. The milk wouldn't last long in this sun. Neither would she at the pace she was going.

Her feet ached and the sunburn on her face stung. She sure would like to rest a spell but she was wary. She knew a body couldn't always tell a coyote by its holler.

Harley suspected all kinds of misdeeds from the man and he'd even gone so far to say Mr. Lafferty had no soul. Harley was grieving his pa and filled with resentment. Even though Mr. Lafferty did seem a mite too friendly, maybe that was just his way.

"Thank you, kindly," she said and she hefted the jug into the back of the wagon.

She picked up her skirt and climbed on board.

Mr. Lafferty shook the reins. The horses started off slowly until he turned them around. When they understood they were going back to town, their steps became more lively.

"I'd like that we could be friends," Mr. Lafferty said.

His request surprised her. Why would he want to be her friend?

"Tell me, Mr. Lafferty. How did you know I'd come out this way?"

"Word gets around," he said and kept his sources to himself.

"I suppose all small towns amount to the same," she said.

Folks thrived on gossip and nobody's business stayed private for long. That Mr. Lafferty knew about her comings and goings made her uneasy. Dory was of the opinion friends didn't keep secrets from one another.

She held on to the side of the seat as the buckboard bounced along the uneven track and thought of Adele. No doubt the town was buzzing like bees about that girl and they'd all have an opinion.

"What else did you hear?" Dory had to know.

"You've got the whore from the saloon living down there in your camp," he said.

So fierce was Dory's loyalty to Adele that her grip tightened. "She's not a whore."

Mr. Lafferty shot her a troubled look. "I'm sorry, Miss Dory, if I offended you. That's what the folks in town call her. That's how she's known to decent folks."

"Decent folks should speak more kindly of those less fortunate."

Mr. Lafferty looked genuinely alarmed. "Don't get yourself riled, lass. I'm sure that girl is in good hands now."

Dory was glad he didn't hold the same attitude as some of the others in town. She hoped he would tell the folks who were set on staying on their side of the line and preventing those on the other side from crossing over about how Adele was being taken good care of in the Watkin' camp.

"I heard that the wagon train is only a few days off," he said.

A tinge of excitement shot through her. "You don't say."

She'd known another wagon train was due but she hadn't expected its arrival this soon.

"A scout rode into town this morning. There's sickness with the party. They're going to set up camp north of us."

The news of sickness didn't surprise Dory. "We'll be leaving as soon as the train is ready and able," she told Mr. Lafferty. "We're going to meet up with my pa and brothers in California."

She didn't know why she told him her plans. More than likely, he already knew.

"California's the land of milk and honey," she continued. She looked at the man for confirmation.

"I reckon that's true," he said.

Dory gazed out at the barren land infested with sagebrush. Weeks ago, she'd had such a strong yearning to leave it behind. Now she was conflicted with mixed emotions. There were friends here and a future that hadn't seemed possible when she'd arrived.

Mr. Lafferty didn't speak much more than pleasantries the next couple of miles. He seemed gentlemanly enough.

She thought of the good men she'd known. Her pa and Uncle Joseph worked hard and were strong-minded. And Pastor Ryland back home. She'd looked up to him all her life. He never backed down from telling the truth and he always had a comforting word for those in need. They'd had good neighbors who'd helped with the harvest, men who tolerated backbreaking labor but always took time for some good-natured joshing at the end of the day.

Those men took care of their families and tried to do what was right.

This here Mr. Lafferty wasn't like them. He didn't break soil or mend fences. She could tell by his smooth hands. He wore his Sunday best suit on a regular working day.

He seemed agreeable, although a mite judgmental but there were failings in every man and woman. He spoke to her adult to adult and she appreciated him doing so.

Dory reckoned to meet all kinds of folks out here in these western lands, even those who spoke foreign. For the first time since they'd left home, she felt proud to be part of the pioneer migration.

When they reached town, Mr. Lafferty slowed his horse to a walk. Few people were outside in the heat of the day.

"You can drop me off anywhere," she said.

"I'm headed for the blacksmith. I can take you that far."

Dory told him the smithy would do fine. She'd only a short walk from there.

They reached the livery and Mr. Lafferty pulled his horses to a stop. The blacksmith wasn't at his forge.

Mr. Lafferty jumped down from his seat. Dory did the same. His hand brushed against hers as their hands reached for the milk jug at the same time. Dory drew back and let him unload the heavy can. He set it down and stood in front of it.

Dory's nerves tingled a warning but she kept calm. "Thank you again for the ride. I best be going to our camp. Ma's expecting me and Adele needs that milk."

Mr. Lafferty wore a funny-looking smile. Dory's insides tightened.

He took a step toward her and Dory backed up. She bumped into the buckboard and he moved closer. Cornered, she moved sideways down the sides of the wagon, her back pressed against the wood. When she reached the end, she bolted.

Mr. Lafferty grabbed her arm and spun her around.

"What do you want?" she said, anger masking her fear. His grip was fierce but she wouldn't show him how much it hurt.

"I like you, Dory. I want you to like me."

His smile turned into a sneer. Dory went cold. She clenched her hands into fists.

"Let me go. Ma will be looking for me." She didn't know if Ma would be missing her or not. Ma was so occupied with Adele she might've lost track of time.

"You'll go when I say you can."

The man drew back his jacket, showing a gun with a pearl handle. Dory hadn't realized he carried a firearm. Most of the men in town didn't. Her pa kept a loaded shotgun under the seat of the wagon but that was in case they came across a fat rabbit out on the open plains.

"You let me pass or I'll yell out so that the whole town will hear," she warned him.

Mr. Lafferty drew out the weapon with his left hand. He held the hard steel against her bosom as if she was an outlaw.

"Do as I say," he said, "and you won't get hurt."

Dory went numb. Her legs wobbled. She wasn't even sure if she could run. She didn't think he'd shoot her but it was hard to say with a man who had no soul.

"You've got a respectable reputation in town," she said. "You wouldn't want folks to change their minds."

"You won't tell 'em."

He pulled her right up against him. She smelled his foul breath and turned her head. She didn't dare look at him.

He used the barrel of his gun to lift apart the buttons on her dress. Dory's heart pounded so loudly her ears seemed ready to burst. She struggled to get away.

He grabbed her around her waist. "Come on sweetheart. Don't play coy with me."

He mashed his lips on her neck. The kiss revolted her and she punched him in the face. Her actions seemed to fuel his desire and she kicked out and connected with his knee. She heard a crunch.

He stumbled back but held the gun on her. He bumped into the milk tin. The lid popped off and milk slopped onto the ground.

Dory lunged at the man and bowled him over. He fell

to the ground. The gun went flying out of his hand. She picked it up. The weapon was heavy but she held it steady using both hands.

"Don't make me shoot you," she said, stepping back.

Mr. Lafferty sat up, holding his knee. He grimaced with pain. "Now listen to me. I was only having some fun. You seem like a girl who likes to have fun."

"You'd no right to talk to me like that," she said to him. "I'm a lady and expect to be treated like one."

"Give me the gun, Miss Dory." He reached out. His hand was bloody. "This was just a simple misunderstanding. Don't make a fool of yourself."

"Seems to me you're the one who's acting the fool. If you give me or my family any trouble, I'll go straight to the decent folks who live here, including Mrs. Jacobs and tell them what kind of man you are."

"Now let's not be hasty It'll be my word against yours."

"Is that so? Mrs. Jacobs thinks you're a gentleman but she'll be persuaded that you're no good when I tell her directly what you tried to do. Word won't take long to get around Ragtown. In fact, if you were smart, you'd hightail it out of the territory. We don't need your kind around here."

She tossed the gun into the smithy's water trough. Mr. Lafferty would have some explaining to do when he fished his weapon out of there. That and a busted knee.

Dory buttoned her shirt, her fingers trembling. She picked up what remained of the milk. The jug was considerably lighter. She left Mr. Lafferty sitting on the ground.

She lugged the pail down to their camp. Adele wore the calico dress Ma had altered for her and she looked pretty and plump standing there by the wagon, her hand on her back. Her flame-colored hair had been braided into a single braid that reached halfway down her back.

Ma saw Dory and climbed the slope to meet her. Her step wasn't as quick as it used to be but her face shone with determination.

"Did you have far to go," Ma examined her closely.

Dory squelched her heated emotions. Ma would guess sure as anything that something had happened.

"Not far. Into the foothills yonder." Dory took a deep breath. "I sure am parched."

Doubt clouded Ma's usual peaceful expression. "I'm sure you are. I'll make some coffee."

Ma helped tote the jug and said nothing about it being less than half full. Dory wasn't ready to explain about what happened with Mr. Lafferty. Even though she'd taken care of that snake and was certain she wouldn't be seeing the likes of him around Ragtown for a while, she didn't want Ma to worry. She'd brought enough worries to their camp. Instead, Dory told her ma about the family and what she'd seen up on the foothills road.

Suddenly they heard a commotion. Two boys from town came running into their camp.

"Harley's a coming from the mountains," they said in unison.

Dory felt as if she was about to be sprung from a bow.

Ma took the pail from her. "Well, go see what he's been up to."

Dory didn't hesitate. She picked up her skirts and started running after the boys. They headed for the road that Pa and her brothers had left on all those weeks ago. In the distance, so far out she could barely make out who was there, came a lone man walking alongside a horse pulling a cart. To her surprise, the cart was full of trees.

"Are you sure it's him?" she asked the boys.

"It's him all right. That's one of his mixed breeds haul-ing that cart."

They continued up the road, closing the distance quick-ly. The boys jabbered on but Dory wasn't listening. She was thinking about how much she'd missed Harley and what in the world was he doing with trees?

It didn't take him long to figure out somebody was coming to meet him. He stopped and pulled down his lavender kerchief. He looked worn out and was covered with trail dust except where his kerchief left a clean path across the bottom half of his face.

By the time she reached him, her heart pounded wildly. Their gazes met. Harley's eyes were red and he wore several days' worth of beard.

She must look at sight but she didn't care. He was back. Every bit of her wanted to wrap her arms around his neck and give him the biggest hug. Only the boys buzzing around prevented her from showing him what she was feeling.

"What'd you bring us?" the boys asked, jumping up to see what was in the wagon.

Harley turned to show Dory what had taken him away all this time. "These are trees for Ragtown. They should grow good with a little tending."

Dory's heart swelled with tenderness. She'd asked for more trees and he'd brought them.

"Where will you plant them?" she asked.

"On my land. I'll plow some ditches for irrigation so they'll have enough water. After a little while, these trees will provide plenty of shade and wood for building."

"Someday I'd like to see your land."

"I'd like for you to see it."

His horse pawed the ground. "I'd better take care of my horse. He's pulled a big load and could use a rest and some feed."

"Looks like you could stand a good meal and a rest as well. Ma's made some corn cakes and everybody says they're the best they've ever tried."

"I could use a hot meal," he said. "And a bath."

He was grinning.

Dory grinned back. She felt as light as a goose feather.

"It'll take up your offer another time," Harley said. "I've got to get these trees in the ground before the roots dry out."

Dory was disappointed but saw the sense in what he'd said. Harley had a practical side that would serve him well in life.

As they walked to town, Harley told her his plans. He explained how the horse was young but had done well navigating the mountain pass like the half-mustang he was. The animal had been able to pull the cart full of trees without much trouble. The emigrants needed these kinds of heavy-duty horses, Harley explained and he meant to provide them.

Dory listened contentedly as his dreams unfolded. Harley expected to accomplish big things with the trees. He envisioned tall trees that would give plenty of shade. He said this twice—a shady place to rest on a hot day.

Dory could almost picture it herself.

His future was set in this town. Ragtown was a place where folks passed through on their way to someplace else, and they needed good horseflesh to take them over the mountains. Harley would do fine with his horse-trading business.

She told him about going over to the Mexican family's ranch and getting goat's milk. She didn't tell him how she'd ridden some of the way back with Mr. Lafferty. He didn't have to be reminded about the low character of the man he was partnered with. She'd leave what happened with that awful man for another day.

She explained about Adele and what the doc had said.

"A baby on the way? What do you reckon?" Harley replied. He said no more.

She appreciated he hadn't made any judgments about what Adele had done.

They arrived at the outskirts of town before she thought it could be possible. The boys ran ahead.

"I sure missed you," she said.

"Do you mean that, Dory?"

"Of course I do. I like talking with you."

"If that don't beat all," he said with a grin. "That's not what I thought you'd miss about me. I thought you'd miss my kissing."

Dory pretended to be shocked. "Why, Mr. Harley Jacobs, how you carry on."

He started laughing and she loved hearing him laugh.

"I'd better go help Ma get dinner started," she said. "Are you sure you won't change your mind and join us?"

She saw the brief look of regret. "It'll have to be another day."

There was moment of connection as they gazed into each other's eyes. At that moment Dory was sure of her heart's desire but how would she convince her ma?

# Chapter Seven

DORY LEFT HARLEY at the blacksmith's tent. What Harley had accomplished seemed like a miracle. A wagon train covered fifteen miles on a good day. At that rate, it took eight days to travel to California across the mountain pass. Harley had gone the distance and come back with that sorry looking horse of his in less than six days. Maybe the time could be cut even shorter for a man riding one of Harley's new breed of horse.

Six days over and back didn't seem so long or so far away. She returned to the camp in a disposition as light and fluffy as Grandma's meringue.

Adele had gathered an armload of brush for the evening fire. Dory felt guilty she'd left them for so long and she hurried to help Adele tote her bundle.

"I seen you with that Harley Jacobs before," Adele said. "Are you sweet on each other?"

Dory looked around to see if her ma had heard. Ma took up a wooden spoon and seemed preoccupied with stirring the washing in the iron pot. She was washing Adele's petticoats in hot water and using the last of the lye soap.

Adele dropped her bundle and brushed off her hands.

"Don't you say anything to Ma," Dory said. "She don't like the idea."

Adele put her finger to her lips. "Don't you worry. I

can keep a secret."

"He brought trees," Dory explained. "He's going to plant them on his land."

"Trees will make this town a pretty place," Adele replied generously.

"Do you think so?" Dory'd been of the same opinion, however.

"This here is a trail town," Adele said, "but someday it'll be fit for good folks like you and your ma."

Dory took her words to heart. They were words of wisdom from someone who'd seen the worst side of this town.

Thinking of what'd happened with Mr. Lafferty, Dory knew it's take a lot more than trees to civilize Ragtown.

THAT NIGHT ADELE'S baby decided to be born.

A low moaning woke Dory and she crawled out of her blankets into chilly air. She wrapped one of the blankets around her shoulders, careful not to wake up her ma. The air was scented with sage and she looked up at the sky with its wealth of stars. She'd never seen anything so beautiful.

As she lit the coal oil lantern, an agonizing cry came from the wagon.

Dory poked her head inside, holding up the light. "Is the baby coming?"

Adele sat up on her elbows. "I reckon. The pain is terrible."

"I'll go fetch Dr. McKinnon," Dory said.

"Don't leave me." Adele screamed and collapsed on the pillow.

That scream just about tore Dory in two, and she climbed into the wagon. Adele looked wild-eyed as she clutched the sides of the bed. Her hair was matted to her forehead.

"There's nothing to be afraid of," Dory said, soothingly. She didn't know if it was the truth but she didn't know what else to say. Adele needed calming. Dory sat down and stroked the wet tendrils off Adele's face.

Dory heard rustling and Ma appeared in the back of the wagon.

"Is it time?" she asked in a whisper.

"Yes, Ma."

Ma pulled herself inside.

"Do the pains come regular?" Ma asked.

"I don't know," Adele replied, breathing hard, "but they're getting worse."

Ma pulled back the blanket Adele clutched for comfort. She looked at Adele's privates.

"I best go fetch the doc," Dory said.

"There's no time and I need you here," Ma said. "Go boil some water and be quick."

Dory set the lantern on a hook and jumped out of the wagon. Thankfully, she'd hauled water up from the Carson before she'd gone to bed. She ladled some from the rain barrel into a tin pot as Adele let out a wail.

The sound most likely woke the dead and frightened Dory so bad she spilled some of the water. She filled the pan again and set it directly on the gray coals.

"I've done what you asked," she said to her ma through the opening in the back.

Adele lay on the bed with her knees up. Dory saw Adele's bottom and averted her eyes. Ma had opened the trunk and took out her best shawl. Adele had come without a stitch of clothing for her baby, an omission that couldn't be helped. Ma handed Dory a pair of scissors from her sewing kit, and a needle threaded with a length of string.

"Put these in the boiling water."

Dory took them.

"And wash your hands."

Dory returned to the fire and tossed the things in the tin pan. There wasn't any soap left and she scrubbed her hands as best as she could with another ladle full of hot water.

Adele's wailing came more frequently now. Her friend suffered beyond what seemed humanly possible and she wondered why birthing had to be so difficult.

"Don't be dawdling," Ma shouted.

Dory scooped the scissors and needle threaded with the long piece of string out of the boiling water using the long-handled wooden spoon. She dropped them in a piece of clean linen and climbed back in the wagon.

Ma pressed on Adele's stomach, telling her to push. Thankfully, Ma knew what to do.

Back home, birthing was done by one of the ladies from a neighboring farm or by a doctor if there was time. What happened in the birthing room was between God and them two. Not even the baby's father took part in bringing his own child into the world.

"You sit at her feet and catch that baby when it's born," Ma said.

"Me?" Dory had serious misgivings she could do such a thing.

"Yes, Dory, your hands are freshly washed. We can't have this baby take sick." Ma's tone left her no choice.

There was blood on the quilt and the smell of blood in the air. Dory was about to witness a miracle. She could only trust in God that her efforts would be enough. She quelled her nervous stomach and demanded more from herself than she'd ever had before.

Adele's eyes showed terror and hair tumbled around her face in disarray as if she'd gone mad.

"Don't you worry," Dory told her. "I won't let you down."

Adele didn't seem to hear. Her face bunched up in a terrible spasm of pain.

"Push," Dory's ma said as she leaned on Adele's stomach.

Adele pushed until there didn't seem to be any push left in her.

Dory saw the most amazing sight. A tiny head appeared with a tangle of dark hair.

"Push harder," Ma said.

Adele drew in a ragged breath and pushed until her face turned beet red.

The baby popped out like a cork out of a bottle. Dory was stunned as she held the wiggling child.

"It's a boy," she cried.

"Wrap that baby up before he takes a chill," Ma said.

Dory grabbed the shawl and wrapped the squalling baby in it. The infant writhed and twisted in her arms as she wiped at the blood off his face. The gentle touch settled him and Dory took satisfaction from such a tiny creature responding to her.

Ma tied the cord with the string and then cut it with the scissors. She took a peek at where the baby had exited.

"Don't look like you tore anything," she told Adele. "You won't be needing my sewing skills."

Adele moaned between clenched teeth and Ma delivered the afterbirth and wrapped it in a towel.

"Now it's over," Ma said reassuringly.

Adele began to smile. Lord knows she hadn't much to smile about in a long while and she reached out for her baby.

"He's handsome," Dory said, settling the infant in his ma's arms.

She beamed at her ma. Ma smiled. The three of them were fit to bust wide open with happiness for the new baby. Dory felt ashamed that she'd held any hard feelings toward Adele.

The baby burst out bawling. The three women laughed at him, a strapping lad with all his fingers and toes. Adele snuggled him against her breast, cooing softly.

"Ain't that like a man, always hungry," Ma said.

"Thank you," Adele said, tears in her eyes. "I don't know how I'll ever be able to repay you."

"Giving that boy a good home is payment enough," Ma said. She picked up her scissors and needle. With one final look of satisfaction, Ma left the wagon. Dory followed.

Ma put her arm around Dory's shoulders. "You did well and proper like you've been taught."

"I was scared."

"We all are when it comes to bringing a new life into the world. Even, I suspect, Dr. McKinnon." Ma turned away.

Dory suspected to hide a tear or two.

"Go fetch him, Dory," Ma said and she sank into her chair.

ADELE CALLED HER baby Homer, a name she was partial to.

Ma lined a basket with the material from Adele's fancy dress and sewed a nightgown out of the washed petticoat. Homer looked like a prince swaddled in such finery.

Homer Brewster liked his feed every two hours or so and Adele never tired of cooing to that baby. Their bond was strong and Dory had no fear Adele would make a good mother.

Harley and his ma were the first to arrive the next morning. Mrs. Jacobs brought nappies she'd put away in her cedar chest. She'd washed them and they smelled like sunshine.

"He's as handsome as me," Harley said. He took the baby but Homer began to cry. With a look of panic, he handed the baby back to Adele.

"My hands are too rough for the little wrangler," he said apologetically.

Adele didn't seem to mind. She sure did look a picture of contentment. Harley's ma got all teary-eyed.

They were surely tears of joy, Dory decided.

"What do you say we go look at those trees?" Harley asked Dory. He was freshly shaved. His mustache had grown and it made him look older. She wondered if it would tickle if he kissed her. She wondered if he intended to kiss her now.

"I wouldn't mind," Dory replied.

They left Harley's ma fussing over Homer and giving Adele advice on raising a young 'un.

When Dory got Harley all to herself, she told him what'd happened and how she'd helped her ma deliver little Homer. She wasn't embarrassed at all and Harley listened intently.

They walked along the riverbank where flat stones made their footing sure and steady. The water rushed past hidden rocks and sparkled off the ones exposed. She hadn't seen a prettier day in a long time.

"What will Adele do now that the baby is born?" Harley asked.

"Stay with me and Ma, I reckon."

"Who do you suppose his pa is?"

Dory stopped. She had her suspicions about his pa but she'd kept them to herself. Adele would let that cat out of the bag when she'd a mind to.

"I never did ask," she said.

Harley picked up a stone and skipped it across the moving water. Something troubled him. "Do you suppose she'd tell you now that the baby is here and safe?"

Most likely he'd noticed the name being the same as his partner's given name. Homer was a fine name, Dory decided and little Homer would do better by it than Mr. Lafferty had done. Harley'd be mad as a hornet if he believed Mr. Lafferty had put Adele in a family way and there was no telling what he'd do to the man. She couldn't let Harley jeopardize his future.

"I don't rightly know," she replied sincerely. "What if she doesn't know?"

Harley frowned. "How could she not know?"

Obviously, Harley hadn't considered the possibility that Adele had been with more than one man.

Dory didn't want to argue. "Maybe she does know but she's not telling."

"That don't rightly seem fair to Homer."

Dory agreed but she was learning that the fairness of the matter didn't hold much water in this untamed land.

Harley turned away from the river and they climbed up a gentle rise until she saw dozens of newly planted saplings a ways off in the distance.

Harley rubbed his hands together. She could see he was mighty proud of what he'd done.

"Is all that land yours?" she asked.

"A good part of it," he said as proud as a rooster.

"You did well choosing," she said. "I haven't seen such like in a very long time."

He made no additions to what she'd said.

She sat down in the tinder-dry grass and gathered her skirt around her legs. Harley sat next to her.

"You know this town's a'changing," he said, "and the folks who live here are changing along with it. There's plenty of opportunity for a man if he's willing to put his back into hard work."

Dory sat still. Her whole being tingled with anticipation for she knew what Harley had brought her out here to say.

"More people will be coming through Ragtown, good people," Harley continued. "Some will want to stay. Others will need fresh supplies to carry on over the mountains into California. Those who stay will build up this town, make something of it."

Dory heard the earnestness in his voice. He was the type of man who wasn't careless with words. She looked at him encouragingly.

He pushed his hat back on his head. He looked at the flawless sky. "I don't expect I'll ever be more than a Ragtown stock man and freighter. It was good enough for my pa and it's good enough for me."

"What are you getting at?" Dory asked. He sure was taking a long time arriving at his destination.

He dropped his gaze to connect with hers. "Your pa isn't here, so I don't rightly know how to proceed proper like."

"Just ask me," she said.

"Dory Watkins, I mean to marry you."

Dory leaned over and kissed him lightly on the mouth. She'd been correct in assuming the mustache tickled. One kiss didn't seem enough but she held off.

"I'd like to be your wife," she said. "I'd like nothing more, but I can't stay in Ragtown."

Harley frowned.

Dory had thought long and hard and could come up with only one solution. "We can get married and you can come out to California with us."

Harley shook his head. "My place is here."

She didn't understanding how he could be attached to one spot. Her temper flared. She'd had it all worked out.

"I'd like to stay here but I can't. I made a promise to my pa that I'd bring Ma safe to California. Now there's Adele. She and little Homer can't manage by themselves. You could come with us. We need someone to drive our wagon."

"But Dory, you're not a kid anymore. You can't expect to stay with your ma and pa forever."

"A promise is a promise. I can't go back on my word."

Harley exhaled. "So your answer is no."

Dory touched his sleeve. "I don't mean to cause you any hurt but I've made up my mind."

She felt like she was back on that mountain road with the rock face on one side and the cliff dropping down to the valley below on the other. She couldn't go against her pa's wishes but her heart ached for Harley's affections.

She rested her head on his shoulder.

Harley stood abruptly. "No, Dory. No need encouraging a fella if you've made your decision."

"Don't speak so harshly," she said, jumping to her feet.

He faced her squarely. "I've said what I came to say. There'll be no more speeches on the matter."

Dory's heart was breaking. He stomped off without another word, his male pride cut to the quick. She wanted to run after him but she didn't. There'd be no compromising by either of them. The matter was settled.

She waited until she collected herself before she made her way back to camp. When she arrived, Adele was sitting in Ma's chair, surrounded by ladies from the town. Word had got out that Homer'd been born and the ladies had come around with gifts that Adele could use including a christening gown. Adele was beside herself with the attention. And the town ladies, to their credit, treated Adele kindly.

"Where's Harley gone off to?" Ma asked, standing beside her and watching the ladies fuss with Homer.

Dory crossed her arms. She felt empty inside. "He left and he's not coming back."

Ma didn't ask why.

# Chapter Eight

EARLY THAT AFTERNOON, Dory went to look for Buck and Gussie who'd wandered off in search of fresh grass. She found the horses grazing by a bend in the river. She picked up a switch to guide them back to their camp and saw a cloud of dust miles off to the northeast. The wagon train would be there by nightfall. She hurried the two horses back, calling out to Ma and Adele.

Ma looked up in alarm. Adele stood beside her, biting her lower lip.

"There's a wagon train coming," Dory said.

Adele clapped her hands. Ma's face glowed. As Dory caught her breath, she realized they'd be leaving soon. She needed to be away from this raggedy old town as soon as possible.

The three women broke out in eager chatter. They couldn't contain their excitement about the new caravan of wagons, each for their own reasons.

Ma had talked it over with Adele and they'd agreed that Adele and Homer would travel with them to California. Adele was going to make a fresh start. Ma was beside herself in anticipation of being reunited with Pa and the boys.

Dory didn't intend to see Harley again. He'd been too stubborn to consider her plan for him to take them to California. No doubt, he'd forget her as soon as they were on their way west.

Soon the jangling and creaking of wagons filled the air with their sweet music. Voices called out to urge their teams forward. Cattle bawled. They smelled the cooling water of the Carson. The ground trembled and birds flew off squawking an alarm. Old Buck pricked his ears forward. He knew what was coming.

When the first wagon appeared over the rise, Dory's eagerness turned to despair. She'd thought this would be a happy day and she wished she could rejoice with the rest of them. She couldn't shake her wretchedness or her foreboding of what must come to pass.

For a long time, she'd believed she was as strong-minded and tough-willed as her pa. Except she'd reserved a tender spot in her heart for a grinning fool of a man. She couldn't forget the all over prickly delight that came with kissing him. Leaving Ragtown would be tougher than she'd bargained for.

The lead wagon turned toward the river and the rest followed until they made a half circle. Like a sigh of relief, the last wagon in the train came to a halt.

Dory made her way to town to find who was in charge and tell him the Watkinses were joining their party. She took the two horses with her to be reshod and left them at the livery. The whole town bustled with energy. When a group of three young men rode into town on weary horses, they were greeted by folks from both sides of the line.

Those fellas were dressed in tattered clothing and looked plumb wore out. They accepted a drink of water gratefully from Mr. Miller. They dismounted and one of the men let his horse drink out of his hat.

Another one shouted out, asking if there was a doctor in the town.

They'd all heard the stories of the illness that felled people on the trail. Those wagons would be set apart like Dory's family's had been. There'd be other tales to tell, of death and hardship, of terrible loss and disappointment.

For now, those three young men showed nothing but gratitude to the folks who'd gathered.

Doc McKinnon arrived quickly to take charge. He wore his coat, hat and a serious expression. He carried his kit under his arm.

The men palavered with the doc. The crowd pushed closer and Dory strained to hear what they said. Everyone was talking at once and Dory couldn't understand a word.

After they'd explained what they'd needed to explain, they got back on their horses and left.

"How many took sick, Doc?" Mr. Miller asked.

"The boy told me there are half a dozen. They've lost a half of dozen more."

Mr. Miller shook his head. "That's bad news."

"They're camped down by the river, a good mile away," Doc said. "We shouldn't be concerned with that much distance between us."

Doc was good at reassuring people. He'd complimented Dory on how well she'd taken care of her ma and on the birthing of Homer, making Dory proud of what she'd done. She understood his encouragement was part of his profession, giving out hope when there often didn't seem to be a reason for any.

"How long they plan on staying?" Mr. Miller asked, anxiously.

"Only a day or two at most. They don't want to be caught by an early snowfall."

Mr. Miller nodded but he looked worried.

Doc cradled his black bag. "I'd better go see what I can

do."

Dory hurried back to their camp to let Ma and Adele know what she'd heard. There'd be time later to find the wagon captain.

Adele nursed Homer, her eyes bright with anticipation. Ma was repacking the trunk.

"They'll be moving off in a couple of days. Right now they need a rest and some good food in their bellies," Dory explained.

Down by the river, Dory saw the three men who'd come into town stripping off their clothes and hollering like a pack of coyotes. She'd never heard such carrying on.

Dory looked away. Ma paid them no mind. No doubt she was wondering about her sons. Most likely those boys hadn't bathed since they left Ragtown.

"I suppose those boys just about had enough of the desert," Ma said.

Adele's face changed abruptly with a cascade of tears.

"Adele, what's the matter?" Dory asked.

"Oh, Dory, I don't know what I'd have done if you hadn't come along when you did."

Dory didn't like Adele upset. "You hush. I did what anybody would've done."

"Me and Homer have imposed on you and your ma long enough." Adele's lower lip trembled.

For the life of her, Dory couldn't understand what'd put Adele into such a fuss.

"You're not imposing," she said sincerely, "and you're coming with us has been decided."

Adele sniffed. "What if those people in the wagon train won't let me go with you?"

Dory couldn't help what folks would think about Adele. They'd sure enough hear about her past. Adele was family now and family stuck together. The Watkinses wouldn't let anybody treat Adele badly.

"Don't you worry," Dory replied. "Nobody's going to turn away a new ma and her babe. When those folks see little Homer, they'll do backflips to take care of him."

Adele wiped her nose with the back of hand. Dory's words seemed to comfort her a little but the girl had seen the worst in human nature and doubted the kindness of strangers.

"Look at how the ladies of Ragtown changed when they heard about Homer," Dory reassured her. "Remember how snooty some of them can be? Didn't their snooty ways go by the roadside when that little babe arrived?"

"I suppose you're right," Adele said.

"Just you watch," Dory said, encouragingly. "We're going to a new life, you and me, to a place yonder beyond those mountains."

Adele wrapped her arms around Dory's waist and gave her a fierce hug. "Thank you. Thank you for everything."

Dory was deeply touched by the girl's gratitude for their help. She hugged Adele back with growing affection for a sister she'd never had. Homer continued to nurse, paying no mind to all the commotion.

Dory'd spoken honestly and from the heart. She'd grown up along the trail. Adults made tough decisions. Even though leaving Ragtown would be one of the biggest decisions of her life, Dory had responsibilities she wouldn't shirk.

Adele's gratitude hardened Dory's resolve. Her family depended on her and she wouldn't let them down.

AFTER GIVING THE folks in the newly arrived wagon train time to take care of their stock and settle into their camp, Dory sought out the boss. Two boys pointed to a man on horseback. He rode a brown gelding with black spots on its rump.

"Our boss is named Seymour," the older boy said.

Dory thanked them and walked over to Mr. Seymour.

"Excuse me, sir," she said.

The trail boss sat forward in his saddle and the leather creaked. He was old, maybe forty and dressed in dirty buckskin. His long mustache needed combing. His morning's breakfast still nested in the stiff hair.

"Who might you be?" he asked, gruffly.

"My name is Dory Watkins. My ma and I were in the Dixon-Ferguson party. Ma got sick and we stayed behind."

"Now you're wishing to join us?"

"The boss said it wouldn't be any trouble. He gave me this letter." She handed the folded piece of paper over to the man.

He didn't read the letter but stuck it inside his flannel shirt.

"We've got two more riding with us," Dory explained. "Adele Brewster and her baby."

"That'll cost ya extra," Mr. Seymour said.

Dory despaired. She hadn't expected an extra charge. "How much more?"

Mr. Seymour scratched his chin. "I won't charge for the young 'un but the woman will cost you thirty dollars."

Dory looked at him with scorn. "That's a mighty hefty price."

"That's the going rate."

"We don't have that kind of money."

"That's not my problem, is it?"

"We can't leave Adele here. She's got nobody to take care of her."

"That's my offer, young lady. Take it or leave it." He kicked his horse and headed toward town.

Most likely to the saloon, Dory decided, watching him go.

Dory was fit to be tied. She'd never met a man who was so mean. There was no chance of coming up with that much money in such a short time. She headed in the same direction, ready to give him a piece of her mind.

The town was filled with weary travelers. They'd washed up and combed their hair. A man played a fiddle on the boardwalk in front of the mercantile. Folks started clapping and some of the young 'uns danced. Dory reckoned it was a tribute to their spirit that even though they must be bone weary, they could still laugh and enjoy the evening.

Sure enough, Mr. Seymour's strange-looking horse was tied to a hitching post in front of the saloon. Dory stayed put on her side of town. She'd no qualms about crossing the line but she didn't dare set foot inside the saloon. The goings-on in that place weren't fit for a lady.

She turned to go back to their camp and she spotted a tall young man who danced with a little girl wearing braids tied with pink ribbons. He was about Adam's age with dark hair and dark eyes. He looked in reasonably good health. The way he swung that youngster around, Dory reckoned he was partial to children.

As she watched them, a notion came to her that needed acting on. She'd told her pa that she'd find a man to drive their wagon. She walked right up to that young man without a second's hesitation.

"Hello," she said. "My name's Dory Watkins."

The young man twirled the little girl around and let her go, giggling.

He touched two fingers to the brim of his wide-brimmed hat. "Howdy, Miss Watkins. Name's Tommy McCade."

"Where are you folks from?" she asked.

"Galena," he said. "Galena, Illinois."

"I know where Galena is. My people are from Ulysses, Kansas."

Tommy McCade took the introductions in stride. They'd both come a long way.

"Well, Mr. Tommy McCade, I won't mince words. My ma and me have need of a driver. We've been staying in Ragtown while my ma recovered from the sickness. My pa and brothers left with our party. Now we're ready to move off with this train. If you're not obliged to somebody else, we'd like to hire you to take us over the mountain."

Tommy McCade pushed his hat back on his head. He had vivid blue eyes and a sweetness about his face that no girl would object to. "I think my pa could spare me."

Right then Harley walked up, his face bunched up in a frown.

"Harley, this is Tommy McCade."

Tommy looked willing enough to shake hands but Harley scowled and acted like he didn't notice.

"Tommy's agreed to drive our wagon when the train leaves," she explained. Harley's face reddened. He mumbled some words and moved on.

Dory excused herself and chased after him. "What's the matter with you?"

"I don't know why you're being friendly with him."

"I told you why. He's going with us to California."

Harley stopped cold in his tracks.

"We need a driver and Tommy agreed." She hesitated. He wouldn't look at her. "Unless you'd like the job?"

Harley snorted like an angry bull. "You know I can't do what you ask. My place is here in this town. My livelihood is here." His gaze pleaded with her. "My roots are here."

"Well, mine aren't," she replied crisply.

"It's goodbye, then," he said.

He left her standing in the middle of the street. That man was prideful but she'd asked him was more than he could do.

Her heart was full of love as he walked away. She wanted to be with him. Her roots would take hold in this town right alongside his. They'd grow this town together.

How would she convince Ma?

Dory found Tommy McCade listening to the fiddle player. He'd leaned up against a post that would be part of the two story mercantile Mr. Miller was building next to his current establishment.

When he saw her, he straightened.

"Look here, Tommy, if you're to hire on as our driver, then you best come down and meet the rest of us."

Tommy looked willing enough. "I suppose it wouldn't hurt."

She brought him down to their camp, still thinking about Harley and how he'd been jealous of her talking to Tommy. How could he think she'd have eyes for anybody else but him?

Ma rested on her kitchen chair looking sleepy. Adele sat on an overturned pail beside her. When Ma saw they had company, she stood.

"Hello," she said kindly.

"Ma, this here is Tommy McCade. Tommy, meet my ma and Adele Brewster."

When Tommy's eyes lit on Adele it was like cupid himself drew back his bow and flung an arrow direct into that boy's heart.

Adele, for her part, looked demure enough. Tommy would find out about her past soon enough but if he was half the man Dory thought he was, then Adele's past wouldn't bother him none and he'd pay no mind to what she'd done at the saloon or who Homer's pa might be.

Tommy sat on the ground by the smoldering campfire and took the cup of coffee Ma brought to him.

"Tommy's agreed to drive our wagon across the mountain into California," Dory said.

Adele clasped her hands together. "How wonderful."

Ma too, looked pleased.

Dory had no doubt Tommy would suit both women fine.

"Have you had your supper?" Ma asked.

"No, ma'am."

"Let me get something for you," Ma said. She rose from her chair and went to the wagon.

"I'll help," Adele said, getting to her feet.

Tommy took a swallow of his coffee as he watched Adele fetch a plate and fork. Dory gathered up her skirt and plopped down in Ma's chair.

"We didn't agree on a wage," Dory said.

"We'll settle up after we get there," Tommy said.

"I appreciate it." Dory shifted in the chair. "I've just been talking to your train boss and he's asking for thirty dollars for Adele to join up with his party."

"Seems like a lot of money," Tommy replied.

"I wish I could help," Adele said behind her.

"I don't know where we're going to find thirty dollars," Ma said.

"Maybe Mr. Seymour will give you credit," Tommy said.

"Do you think so? You know I'm good for your wages once the wagon train arrives in California but Mr. Seymour needs convincing."

Ma ladled out a generous helping of rabbit stew onto Tommy's plate. "Pa won't like it. He nearly died of shame asking my brother for a loan to buy the oxen."

"This won't be borrowing," Dory said. "We're just delaying payment for services for a bit. You know Pa will make good our debts as soon as we arrive."

Tommy gulped down some stew before he spoke. "Don't you worry. I'll ask Mr. Seymour to give you a line of credit like he'd done other folks."

Dory looked into the fire, grateful for Tommy's help. Thanks to him, they wouldn't have to fret about money.

"Thank you, Tommy," she said. "A line of credit will be appreciated."

She was happy for Adele and that handsome baby of hers. Providence had put Tommy and her together and they wouldn't need any nudging from anyone to start a new life.

What about Dory Watkins? Watching Tommy and Adele making eyes at each other, Dory wished her own destiny was as certain.

TOMMY SAID HIS farewells and goodnights and left with a promise that he'd return in the morning to help with the horses. Adele yawned and said she should be retiring for some sleep before Homer woke. Dory picked up the bucket and left her ma sitting on her kitchen chair humming.

Dory drew a pail of water from the river for the morning. When she got back, Ma was waiting.

Dory emptied the pail of water into the rain barrel and set it down. She took a seat next to her ma.

"Tommy told us the wagon train will only be stopping for a couple of days," Ma said as she stirred the dying embers with a stick.

"They have to get over those mountains before the snow starts," Dory replied.

"Imagine, after all this heat, we might be trudging through a snowfall," Ma said.

Dory looked at her ma. The orange glow of the fire flickered across her face. She was wise and hard-working, two traits Dory had aspired to all her born days.

"What's troubling you, daughter?"

"I want to stay here in Ragtown with Harley, if he'll still have me."

Her ma smiled. "I know."

"I can't break my promise to Pa."

Ma took her hand and gave it a squeeze. "You've kept your promise."

Dory didn't think she'd heard right. Either that or her ma was talking crazy.

"You're strong. You took good care of me. You saved Adele and her baby. You fulfilled your promise to your pa by being the woman you are."

Dory was proud to hear her ma say so. "I love you, Ma. I surely do."

"You're all grown up, Dory," Ma smiled gently. "A woman cleaves with a man, starts her own family and makes a place in the community. That's all I ever wanted for you. As much as I expected that one day you'd take your place beside a husband, I didn't think I'd lose you so soon."

She wrapped her arms around her ma's neck. "Oh, you haven't lost me. Harley's new breed of horse can cover the trail in no time. We will come out to California and see you and Pa and the boys."

Big, fat tears welled up in Ma's eyes. "Look at me blubbering."

Dory wiped her own eyes with the back of her hand. Both she and Ma knew the possibility of seeing each other again was slim. She'd said many goodbyes in the past six months but this one, Dory knew, would be the hardest.

After a while, Ma drew her shawl closer and stood.

"I'd better get my rest. Tomorrow will be a busy day."

Dory looked up at her. "I almost forgot. Tomorrow's my birthday. Well, there's no cause to make a fuss."

"For a birthday, maybe not, but there's to be a wedding, isn't there?" Ma said. "I don't intend to miss the wedding of my only daughter."

EARLY THE NEXT morning, Dory found Harley helping the newly arrived pioneers set up a stockade for their livestock. Head bowed, he dug a hole for a fence post and swatted at a pesky horsefly that wouldn't give him any peace.

Dory couldn't help but giggle.

Harley saw her and leaned against his shovel.

"I expect there's something we need to talk over," she said.

Harley's look of surprise gave her some satisfaction. He'd learn soon enough a woman had a right to change her mind.

He brushed off his hands and handed the shovel to one of the other fellas.

They walked down to the Carson. The dried-up sagebrush snapped under foot. When they came to a shady spot next to a twisted cottonwood tree, they stopped.

"Say what you gotta say," he said.

"I figure Ragtown is as good a place as any for settling down in, providing the right kind of man is my by side," she replied.

That hangdog look left him.

"Are you willing?" she asked.

Harley stepped closer. "I think it best you let me do the asking."

"I'm waiting, Harley Jacobs."

Harley settled his big hands around her waist. "I'm needing a wife."

"I'm agreeing to take you up on your offer."

He drew her to him and planted a solid kiss on her lips.

DORY WAS BURSTING with happiness. Ma had brought along her wedding dress and worked all morning to lengthen the hem. Otherwise it fit Dory to perfection. Adele had helped her button up the back and declared she'd never seen anyone prettier.

When Dory looked in the little square mirror, she was no longer the girl who'd set out west all those months ago, but a woman.

That evening, on Dory Watkins' eighteenth birthday, the largest wedding Ragtown had ever seen took place on the spot where they'd build a church one day. Everyone was decked out in their finest, even the trail boss, Mr. Seymour, who'd taken a bath and trimmed and combed his unruly mustache. He'd seen fit to let Adele take Dory's place so there wouldn't be any need to ask for the loan of thirty dollars.

When Dory caught sight of Harley in his best suit and his hair slicked back with store-bought oil, she knew she'd made the right decision.

Tables had been set out and food brought by the townsfolk. The fiddler provided music for the Virginia Reel and more waltzes than a body could count.

She and Harley would help to build a community, a place their children could thrive in and continue. They'd change the name of the town to one more fitting a place with permanence. The imaginary line down the middle of town wouldn't be necessary.

Dory knew there was good in people and a bent in some to go astray. That much didn't change no matter where a body planted herself.

All kinds would be welcome as long as they abided by the law.

Ragtown was going to be more than a trail town. It was going to be a place called home.

Dear Readers,

Come take a journey with me to Edwardian England and the American West where feisty heroines and the men they love find adventure and their happily ever after.

I write romance and strive to infuse each character with the personal courage and commitment to take the journey of self-discovery that will make them worthy to love. How my characters arrive at their destinations continues to amaze me.

My background is as American as apple pie. I was born and raised in northern Michigan, graduated from the University of Michigan, and worked as a Peace Corps Volunteer in Kenya.

Today my husband and I live in San Diego, the place of my heart, close to our beautiful children and grandchild.

I welcome your comments and I hope you'll join me on social media. Let me know what you are reading and what kinds of books you like.

With thanks,
Sarah

Facebook: facebook.com/sarahrichmondwriter
Twitter: twitter.com/srichmondwriter
Goodreads:
goodreads.com/author/show/1725233.Sarah_Richmond

# Books about the American West by Sarah Richmond

Dulcie Crowder Gets Her Man

Brides of Serendipity
Courtin' Dory
Barrett's Law
Rosy
Angels with Dirty Faces

# Also by Sarah Richmond

Rose Adagio
Past Forgetting
A Most Ineligible Suitor
Do Be Sensible, Miss Wynchcomb
A Perilous Proposal: Book One in the House of Caruthers
series
A Secret Engagement: Book Two in the House of
Caruthers series
A Wayward Wedding: Book Three in the House of
Caruthers series
Running on Empty
Mrs. Pratt's War

Find out more at www.SarahRichmond.com

www.ingramcontent.com/pod-product-compliance
Lightning Source LLC
Chambersburg PA
CBHW030545130626
46552CB00006B/2433